FACES OF DARKNESS

By

Steven A. McKay

Copyright © 2019 All rights reserved

All rights reserved. No part of this book may be reproduced,
in whole or in part, without prior written permission from the copyright holder.

CHAPTER ONE

Croftun, Northern England
October, AD 1329

"My lady, are you all right? My lady?" The serving girl knocked on the door again, and, hearing nothing from within the chamber, tried the latch. It was bolted from the inside, and now the servant felt a chill run down her back. She knew her mistress was in the room, so why wouldn't the lady answer her calls or open the door? It was completely out of character. Yet not, perhaps, entirely unexpected…

Once more the servant hammered on the door, louder this time, and shouted, even using the mistress's name. "Isabella, please open the door."

It was fruitless, and the shadows cast by her flickering candle now seemed weirdly sinister, so the girl turned and ran along the corridor to the kitchen, finding it invitingly warm and well-lit in comparison to the cold, gloomy corridor. The old cook, Reynardine, was hard at work preparing the evening meal just as he'd done in the manor house for decades.

"What's wrong, Anne?" the man demanded, seeing the fear written on the serving girl's face, her candle extinguished and exuding only black smoke in place of its expected cheery light. "Are you hurt?"

"No, it's the lady. Her door's bolted and she won't answer me. I fear something is wrong, Reynardine. Come with me, you must open it so we can check on her."

The cook may have recently passed his sixtieth year, but he was still wiry and strong. Frowning, he lifted the large serrated knife he used to cut fresh loaves and gestured for the girl to relight her candle.

"Lead the way then, lass," he said, and his presence gave Anne courage. Following his example, she took a heavy wooden rolling pin and held it before her as if it was a longsword and she was on her way to battle, then she headed back out into the corridor.

They hurried to the lady's door and this time Reynardine knocked, his lean fist thumping loudly on the oak, making Anne cringe. If this was all a mistake, they would both be in trouble for causing such a fuss.

Still no sound came from inside though, and the old cook eyed the serving girl uncertainly.

"Maybe we should fetch the master?"

Anne shook her head. "He's away in the fields overseeing the repairs to the fences that blew down in the storm last night. She might need our help *now*."

"Well, it's bolted on the other side," Reynardine hissed, trying the door just as Anne had done shortly before. "What do you want me to do? Smash it down?"

The girl shrugged her shoulders unhappily. "Aye, I suppose so. With everything that's been happening—"

"Nothing's been happening," Reynardine spat, although his anxious expression and tightly clutched knife suggested he believed otherwise.

"*Something* has been happening," Anne replied firmly. "Whatever the truth of the lady's claims. She might be lying dead in there…"

Her voice trailed off as the implications of her words finally sank in. What she'd said seemed to galvanise Reynardine though, and after one last fruitless attempt to rouse Lady Isabella, he leaned back, muttered a prayer to the Blessed Virgin, and kicked the door.

It was made of thick oak, and braced with iron, but the bolt apparently hadn't been crafted with the same strength, as the door burst open at that first blow.

Anne, glanced at the cook, fear written all over her plain features.

With a wavering sigh, Reynardine walked slowly into the room, knife held ready at his side, prepared for...what?

"Saints preserve us," he muttered, eyes drawn to the prone figure beside the bed. Still, he stood his ground, eyes scanning the rest of the room for signs of intruders until, satisfied, he hurried across to Lady Isabella de Courcy.

"Oh, God," Anne whimpered, rooted to the spot by the door. "Is she alive? Who could have done that to her?"

Reynardine crouched next to his mistress and, although as a cook he was used to blood and carving dead flesh, his complexion was deathly white as he took in the sight before him.

Face down, sprawled on the ground, Lady Isabella lay unmoving, with something tied around her neck. Most shocking of all, though, was her left hand. A short-bladed knife had been forced through it, into the wooden floorboard beneath, and attached to that was a fragment of cloth or paper.

"Is she dead?"

Reynardine gazed at his mistress's still form and seemed to have no idea what to do. He knelt there, motionless, gazing at the prone woman as if lost in a dream.

"Reynardine," the serving girl demanded, and her tone shocked the cook into life again.

"She's alive," he replied, and his voice, in contrast to Anne's, was low and calm. "I can see her back rising and falling. Bring me the towel, there, and some water. Hurry."

Glad to be offered some direction, the girl obeyed, fetching the things he'd asked for and carrying them over as the cook loosened the strip of fabric around the mistress's throat.

He tore the proffered towel into three strips, and the servants gazed at one another, this terrible event somehow forming a bond between them. And then Reynardine reached down and slowly drew the dagger from his mistress's hand, although it needed a tug at first, to free it from the floorboards.

Anne required no guidance now – she knew how to clean a wound, and she did so with one strip of the towel, although there was surprisingly little blood from such a bad injury. Reynardine examined the piece of paper that was still attached to the blade of the dagger – there was writing on it, but he put it aside without a word.

Lady Isabella moaned softly but didn't move until Anne had finished cleaning and binding her wound. Only when Reynardine dipped the last strip of towel into the water and used it to wipe the mistress's brow did Isabella's eyes flutter open.

"You're all right now, my lady," Reynardine said, cradling her head and speaking in soft tones to reassure the injured woman and stave off any fits of hysteria. "Just you lie there until you feel like you can move, and then we'll get you into your bed and you can have a nice rest."

Tears suddenly filled Isabella's eyes and she began to shake, from both her ordeal and the chill in the room.

"You're safe, my lady," Anne repeated, forcing a smile onto her face although she was crying now as well. "We'll take care of you."

They remained in silence for a long time and Reynardine placed a blanket from the bed around the lady until she seemed to gain control of herself, the shaking and sobbing both passing, to be replaced by a vacant gaze which was almost as unsettling.

"What happened, my lady?" Anne asked, instantly wishing she hadn't as Isabella's face screwed up and her body was wracked with sobs once again.

"I don't remember," she cried, and the despair in her eyes was enough for Anne.

The serving girl ran from the room, rolling pin in hand, to fetch the master from the fields.

CHAPTER TWO

The Franciscan friar known as Tuck grinned as he took the mug of warmed ale from his host in one hand to go with the piece of buttered bread in the other. His cheery expression disappeared though, at the sound of footsteps pounding along the hallway outside the room. Instinctively, having spent so much of his recent life as an outlaw, his hand fell to his side, where he carried a heavy cudgel within the folds of his grey robe.

He glanced at his companion, who had also placed a hand on the pommel of his sword. If the hasty footsteps did presage trouble, Tuck and his companion, the bailiff Little John, would be well prepared for it.

"Excuse me," said Sir Adam de Courcy, turning away from them to throw open the door. Outside, in the hall, a serving girl almost charged straight into the nobleman, a rolling pin flying from her hand to clatter on the floor as she stopped.

"Master," she gasped in surprise. "I thought you were still out in the fields—"

"I came back to receive some visitors from Wakefield, Anne," said de Courcy, frowning as he took in the breathless, frightened girl. "Where are you going in such a hurry?"

"Forgive me sir," Anne cried, and Tuck could tell from her voice that she was close to becoming hysterical. "It's the mistress."

"What of her? Damn it, girl, spit it out. What's happened to my wife?"

The servant began to cry and the friar got to his feet, coming over to gently nudge his host to one side and, taking Anne's hands in his, he smiled kindly at her.

"Calm yourself, lass. Is there danger?"

"No," she replied. "At least I don't think so. Maybe. The mistress has been attacked. In her chamber."

Without another word, de Courcy started running in the direction Anne had come from. Tuck hurried after him, as did Little John and the terrified girl. If there was an intruder within the manor house, the friar thought, grasping his cudgel firmly, they had picked the wrong day to come.

De Courcy was a younger man than Tuck, and Little John felt obliged not to leave behind the servant, so the nobleman made it to his wife's chamber before the rest of them. When the friar came in through the open door he saw Sir Adam kneeling beside the bed, the Lady Isabella clutching a bandaged hand in obvious pain and distress, and a man in cook's clothing standing in the corner with a knife in his hand.

Tuck assumed the old cook was not the attacker, but rather a colleague of the serving girl.

"Did you see him, Isabella?" the nobleman was demanding, in a hard tone of voice which Tuck felt inappropriate given the young woman's ordeal. It wasn't his place to interfere in the dynamic of their relationship though, and, unbidden, he began to inspect the room for signs of what had taken place.

"No," the lady sobbed. "Please, Adam, my hand is really hurting. Can you fetch me something for it?"

"Anne," de Courcy said irritably. "Go and fetch some wine for the lady, hurry."

"No," broke in Isabella, eyes wide. "I can't stay in this room another moment." Tuck turned to look at her and realised there was a length of fabric tied around her neck, which also bore tell-tale red bruising. Clearly, she had suffered a most violent assault – no wonder she wanted away from the scene of the crime.

"John," he said. "Could you help Lady Isabella to the room we came from? Would that be acceptable, Sir Adam? Aye? Good. Anne will make the place comfortable, with some unwatered wine to numb the pain a little and..." He stood next to the bed as the injured woman rose to her feet. "Fear nothing, my lady. If the person who did this to you is still around, Little John will deal with them."

"You can be sure of that," rumbled John who, at over six-and-a-half feet, had to stoop to avoid hitting his head on the doorframe. "You're safe with me, my lady."

The small party moved away along the corridor, leaving Tuck with de Courcy and the anxious cook.

"What happened, Reynardine?" asked the nobleman, and his voice was free of the irritation with which he had addressed his wife Tuck noted. Instead, de Courcy sounded merely tired.

"Anne couldn't get the door open, my lord," the cook said, eyes respectfully downcast although there was a hardness to his tone that made Tuck wonder how much the man cared for his master and mistress.

"So she came to fetch me. There was no sound from inside the room when I got here so…I'm sorry, but I thought it best to break the door open."

De Courcy waved a hand, dismissing Reynardine's fears over replacing the damaged bolt.

"When we came in, Lady Isabella was face-down on the floor there." He gestured, and Tuck moved across to examine the floorboards, noting the gouge in the wood immediately. "There was a scarf or something tied around her neck, choking her. I loosened it so she could breathe again but, her hand…" His voice trailed off, and Tuck pointed to the damaged floor.

"Her hand was here?"

The cook looked at the friar in bemusement, as if seeing him for the first time, and then he glanced to de Courcy, who nodded.

"Answer his question, Reynardine, it's all right. Brother Tuck is here with the bailiff."

Little John was an official representative of the Sheriff of Nottingham and Yorkshire – a lawman – and the old man's eyes widened as he realised now who the two visitors were. Everyone in England had heard of them after all.

"Right you are, sir," the cook said a little hoarsely, then, taking a deep breath, continued with his story. "The lady's hand was…pinned to the floor I suppose you could say, with the blade there."

"My God," de Courcy muttered, shaking his head as he lifted the short knife from the bedside table.

"That piece of paper was attached to it, my lord."

Tuck went over to the window and looked out. The glass hadn't been broken, and the latch was in place, so the attacker had not entered the room via this route. And yet, the servants had found the door bolted from the inside…

He turned back to gaze at de Courcy, who had just muttered a most un-Christian oath as he inspected the bloody scrap of paper that had been attached to his injured wife's hand.

"What does it say, my lord?"

The nobleman looked up, his face pale, and handed the note to the friar, who felt a chill run down his back as he too read the message from the mysterious attacker.

In crude handwriting, was an unmistakeable threat, which the letter writer had thankfully failed to carry out successfully on this occasion:

"NOW YOU MUST DIE, WHORE".

CHAPTER THREE

"And you say this has been going on for months, Sir Adam?"

De Courcy nodded wearily. "Perhaps a couple of years, all told."

Little John let out a soft whistle of amazement and Tuck understood why. He, John and de Courcy were walking in the well-tended gardens around the manor house, searching for clues that might explain how their mysterious visitor had gained access to Isabella's bedchamber.

The bailiff was there that day simply to collect a fine that had been laid against one of the workers within the household. He'd brought his old friend Friar Tuck along for a bit of company, and because it was hardly advisable to go wandering about the countryside carrying money. Even one as feared as Little John – former outlaw, and member of Robin Hood's legendary gang – might be waylaid by robbers looking for the coins in his purse.

De Courcy, a small, sturdily built man of forty years, had met them as they approached the house and, knowing them from the village, had offered them food and drink as the weather had turned quickly this year and frost lay thick on the ground already.

Yet, despite that, there seemed to be no suspicious footprints discernible either in the mud or the frost outside any of the windows of the manor house. Where had the attacker come from and, more worryingly, where had they gone? It was possible the man, for it was a man according to Lady Isabella, was hiding within the estate or even the house, waiting for another chance to complete his murderous task.

Perhaps de Courcy had that very thought in his head as they finished checking the ground close to the house, for he looked up at the sky and addressed John. "Bit early in the year for it, but it looks to me like snow is on its way. You and the friar should spend the night here, bailiff. You don't want to be caught in a blizzard out there on the road."

In truth, John simply wanted to get home to Wakefield and see his family, but Tuck, sensing his reticence, plucked at his sleeve.

"That sounds like a good idea, Sir Adam," the friar said, before his friend could object. "We would be grateful of your hospitality and perhaps I might even question your wife more about her ordeal?"

The nobleman shrugged. "You can go and do it now if you like – I'm sure she'll be glad of the company. The bailiff and I will continue our search of the grounds."

"Fair enough, Sir Adam," John agreed, although he shot Tuck a black look. "We can question your workers in the fields and workshops, see if they know anything. Maybe one of them saw the intruder lurking about."

The nobleman led John north, to the field that ran parallel to the main road, where some workers were repairing fences, while Tuck headed back into the house, rubbing his gloved hands together to bring some warmth back into them.

"Ah, Friar Tuck. Come in." Lady Isabella had regained some of the colour in her cheeks and she looked much better for her medicinal cup of wine. "Will you sit with me? Yes? Then you may go, Robert, and be about your duties. Thank you."

The tall man she'd addressed nodded politely to Tuck and went off about his business which, the friar guessed from the smell that clung to him, was in the stables.

"Robert was guarding me while you were all outside," the lady said, slightly embarrassed by the admission. "Take a seat, please."

Tuck sat down but shook his head as he did so. "I don't blame you for wanting protection, my lady. It's only prudent after your terrible experience this morning."

She smiled and the friar properly took in her appearance for the first time. Blonde-haired, with a pretty face and a slim figure, she would be little match for a strong man intent on harming her.

"I'm afraid I still feel rather weak," Isabella told him, gesturing towards the food and drink sitting on the table from earlier. "Feel free to refresh yourself with whatever you like, though. Hopefully you have a better appetite than I do after…"

Tuck was not one to refuse hospitality, but he wanted to focus on questioning the lady for now and stuffing his face with ale and sweetmeats would hardly be conducive to that end. A little sadly, he shook his head.

"Refreshments can wait, my lady. I was wondering if you could tell me more about your ordeal. If it's not too upsetting for you? It was only a short while ago after all—"

Isabella broke in and there was a strength to her voice Tuck hadn't expected. "What do you want to know?"

"Can you tell me what happened?" he asked. "From the beginning I mean."

She looked into the fire, as if gathering her thoughts, and then she said, "This morning I was sewing a tablecloth – it's been so cold recently that I've been thinking ahead to the forthcoming yule celebrations, for which I always use that particular cloth. It has a pretty holly and ivy design embroidered along it you see. Oh, I love Christmas time, don't you?" Her eyes sparkled like an excited child's as she glanced at the friar, but her expression grew dark once more as she went on with her tale. "There were a couple of small tears in the fabric, so I was mending it in a room near the kitchen. That particular room has a large east facing window, making it pleasant in the mornings when the sun comes up. But, as you know, today was overcast and, despite a small fire in the hearth, I felt rather cold. So, I went to my bedchamber for an extra woollen cloak…"

Her voice trailed off and a look of fear passed across her delicate features before she continued.

"You've seen the room – there is a window, but it's in shadow most of the day and rather gloomy. I walked in and…I felt something being put around my neck, so tight that I couldn't breathe or even cry for help." Unconsciously, her hand reached up to touch the bruises on her throat and her eyes dropped to the ground. A piece of blue fabric lay there.

"Did you struggle?" Tuck said, lifting the scarf but finding no clues upon it.

Isabella nodded. "I tried, but he was very strong, Brother Tuck. The pressure was all pulling me down. I could not fight back, despite every fibre of my being screaming at me to do so."

Tuck understood exactly what she meant. He had been a champion wrestler in his younger days, before he became a clergyman, and the choking move she described was well known to him. It was very difficult to break out of, even if you knew what you were doing.

"Did he say anything to you?" he asked.

"Nothing. Not that I can remember anyway. I passed out, and, when I woke up Anne and Reynardine were in the room with me and my hand was..."

She winced painfully and they sat for a while, both lost in their thoughts, with only the cheerful crackling of the fire disturbing the silence.

It did not make sense Tuck thought. Something in her story didn't quite add up.

"Forgive me, my lady," Tuck said at last, "but your cook…"

"What about him?" Isabella replied.

"Is he trustworthy? Perhaps I imagined it, but I felt there was something in his voice when he was talking to us. Anger maybe?"

The noblewoman gazed at him, surprised. "You are very perceptive," she replied at last. "Reynardine has been with my family for many years and always served us loyally. He has never approved of my marriage though. I don't think Adam has ever noticed, and I'm amazed that you picked up on it so quickly. But yes, poor old Reynardine has been upset with me ever since the day I was wed."

CHAPTER FOUR

At that moment, the door burst open and de Courcy strode in without knocking, Little John at his back. From their expressions it was clear they'd found no clues to the lady's attacker.

"I see you've still had nothing to eat, Brother Tuck," de Courcy said, noting the as yet untouched food on the table. "You must be as hungry as I am after all this carry on. Dig in, man. You too, bailiff." With those words, the nobleman helped himself to a plate of meat, bread, cheese and a mug of ale. He didn't bother warming the drink, being rather red in the face, no doubt from striding around his estate on a wild goose chase. His expression softened, however, as he looked at Lady Isabella lying on the low couch, pale and drawn, and he moved to her side, placing a hand on her forehead.

Tuck decided it would be best not to continue his conversation with Lady Isabella just then, suspecting he might find her more forthcoming if they were alone.

"I'm tired, Adam," she said. "And I don't feel very well."

The nobleman nodded. "That's to be expected, my dear, given your injuries. Get some sleep then, and we'll have your injured hand properly dressed when you wake up. Meanwhile," he gestured towards Tuck and John. "The three of us will stand guard over you. You'll be quite safe."

The young woman forced a smile and then closed her eyes as de Courcy returned to the table to finish his meal.

The men ate and drank in silence and their presence seemed to bring solace to Lady Isabella, who was soon fast asleep, the fear and anguish that had lined her face now gone, replaced by a serenity that Tuck found quite touching.

"You found no tracks," the friar said, pitching his voice low so as not to wake Isabella. "No clues?"

John shook his head and wiped a breadcrumb from his grizzled brown beard. "Nothing out of the ordinary."

"I'm glad you two happened to be here," de Courcy said with a sigh, placing his emptied plate back onto the table and refilling his ale mug. "Your presence has helped my wife immensely. I only wish…" His voice trailed off and he glanced towards the sleeping lady, a frown darkening his face.

When it became clear he would not finish whatever he'd started to say, John spoke up.

"Sir Adam, you mentioned earlier," he said, "that this had been going on for years. Can you tell us more?"

De Courcy stood up and walked over to the hearth, placing another log into the flames from the small pile at the side. Using a poker to stir up the smouldering embers beneath the fresh fuel, he nodded.

"Indeed. For perhaps two years now, my wife has reported being…tormented, by some unknown person who seems to know her every movement. Today is very worrying though." Fire brought back to life, de

Courcy turned to face them again. "This is the first time she has been attacked. Or injured at least."

"I see." Tuck sipped his ale and stretched his legs out towards the fire, enjoying the warmth. Although not yet fifty, his body had endured a lot of wear and tear during his life and his joints did not appreciate the recent cold weather. "And yet, her door and window were, apparently, bolted from the inside."

De Courcy raised his eyebrows but said nothing.

"Perhaps you could give us an account of the things that have happened previously, Sir Adam?" Little John asked, pulling his own chair closer to the fire for, as the nobleman had predicted earlier, it had begun to snow outside, and a chill wind rattled the window.

Despite the noise, Tuck knew from his earlier inspection that the glazing, in this room as well as Lady Isabella's, was in good repair. Apparently the de Courcys' estate earned enough each year to allow for such luxuries. Most houses in the surrounding towns and villages did not have glazed windows, merely wooden shutters which had to be closed practically all day during the winter.

This room in the manor house was, as a result, an unusually comfortable one to Tuck and John, whose time as outlaws, living in the forests even at this harsh time of year, was now a rapidly fading memory since their pardons a few years before.

"The first thing my wife reported to me," de Courcy began, "was, like I say, around two winters ago. She had retired to bed early and was alone for I had been conducting some business in Pontefract and hadn't returned home yet. She fell asleep but was awakened by a noise outside." He looked across at Lady Isabella. "As she lay there, wondering what she'd heard, a man's voice came to her."

"Did she recognise it?" Tuck asked, receiving a shake of the head from the nobleman in return.

"No, the man apparently disguised it, using a guttural, almost demonic tone as he…" De Courcy broke off, embarrassed. "Described what he would like to do to Isabella within the bed."

Little John murmured an oath, but Tuck gestured for de Courcy to continue.

"Disgusting things this man said to her, and she lay there, too frightened to move or reply to the unseen devil outside. Eventually, I returned home and she related the tale to me. I, along with some of the servants, searched the grounds, just as we did today, bailiff. And, again, like today, we found no trace of any interloper."

"Your wife appeared genuinely frightened though?" Tuck asked.

"Oh, yes," de Courcy replied. "She certainly seemed to believe it had been no mere nightmare."

"And you?"

The nobleman's eyes narrowed, and he chewed the side of his cheek momentarily. "Like I say, we could find no evidence of any intruder on the grounds. No footprints outside the window, no reports of anyone lurking in the area – nothing. I believed her though. Why should anyone make up such a disturbing tale?"

"Why indeed," Tuck agreed, shaking his head sadly.

"What other things happened before today's incident, Sir Adam?" Little John asked.

De Courcy walked over to gaze through the window, onto the gardens which were now carpeted with a thin layer of soft white snow. When he spoke again his voice sounded hollow, as if he was heartily fed-up with the whole business.

"The voice, in the night, when Isabella was in a room alone, threatening her. It happened more than once."

"No-one else ever heard this voice?" John asked, frowning.

De Courcy turned back to them and shook his head. "No-one."

"That proves nothing, of course," Tuck interjected. "If this man harassing her is clever, he presumably watches for the most opportune moment to strike without being caught."

De Courcy raised his eyebrows and shrugged. "Of course."

"Anything else, my lord?" John went on. "Other than the voice?"

"Once, Isabella claimed someone tried to open the window. She heard it rattling and, thinking it was the wind, went over to make sure it was latched properly. She claims a man was outside, in the dark, although he was veiled in shadows so she couldn't recognise him."

John grunted. An all too familiar pattern was developing here.

"The servants were roused by the sound of glass breaking, as was I, and we all rushed to Isabella's chamber. I was first to reach her, and found her in great distress, unsurprisingly."

"The intruder smashed the window?"

De Courcy nodded in reply to Tuck's question. "Apparently so. However—" He stared out into the snowy grounds once again "—there was as much glass on the inside of the room as there was outside, as the servants will confirm."

"Meaning whatever smashed the window could have come from either side," John muttered in disgust. "The more of this tale I hear, the more the mystery deepens."

"Did you find a missile?" Tuck asked. "A rock perhaps? An arrow?"

"No," de Courcy said. "The servants took candles and went outside, finding several rocks that might have been thrown through the glass from inside the chamber. I checked the room and found only a brass candlestick lying on the floor."

"It had been knocked over by the lady in her fright?"

"No, Brother Tuck," the nobleman said, meeting his eyes with what might have been interpreted as a sardonic smile. "Isabella insisted it had gone missing from her room two days before. She had not mentioned it at the time because she didn't want the servants to be reprimanded for stealing it."

The three men sat in silence, as de Courcy refilled their ale mugs from the jug on the table and handed them back. Tuck got up, somewhat stiffly, and placed the poker in the hearth for a few moments, before plunging its tip into his drink with a fragrant sizzling that filled the room.

"Is that all, Sir Adam?" John asked, shaking his head as Tuck offered him the poker.

"No. There were messages left for Isabella in various places. Threats – written in the condensation on a window, or scratched onto a door, or on a scrap of paper left where she would find it."

"What did they say?"

The nobleman huffed and narrowed his eyes, trying to remember the hateful words. "You can probably guess," he said. "*'I'll get you one night'. 'You're dead Isabella'*. There was one around her birthday last year which was very strange: '*Last days. Warning. Run. Death. Happy Birthday.*'" He shivered and looked at Tuck. "Something like that anyway."

"Do you still have any of them?"

"No, my wife found them distressing, naturally, so we destroyed them or painted over them whenever they appeared."

"That is unfortunate," the friar muttered. "We might have gained some insight from them."

"I saw them all, friar," de Courcy retorted irritably, not pleased by the criticism in Tuck's words. "There was nothing to be gleaned from them."

His hard tone made the sleeping lady start, and she awoke, wide-eyed and frightened.

"It's all right, Isabella," her husband murmured, moving across to gently brush a strand of hair from her over her eyes. "You're quite safe. You can spend the night here. I will have Anne sleep on the other couch, while the bailiff and the friar – if they are agreeable – can sleep in the adjoining room."

"Of course," Little John said, rising to his full height and smiling reassuringly at the noblewoman. "No intruders will disturb you again while we're here, you can be sure of that."

Tuck nodded agreement. "We will take turns to sleep so one of us will be awake and alert all through the night."

"Like old times, eh, Brother Tuck?" said de Courcy, referring to the two friends' history as outlaws. His tone was neutral again, and it was impossible to tell if he was being critical or merely making conversation as he shepherded them from the room and into the one next door.

There were two beds already made up, and a low fire in the hearth to take the worst of the chill from the air. With a tight smile, their host bid them sleep well, thanked them for their help that day, and left them alone.

"What do you think's going on here?" Little John asked softly, when they were sure de Courcy had gone. "It's a bloody weird business, isn't it? The lady must be shitting herself."

Tuck pursed his lips thoughtfully and removed his boots, eager to get beneath the warm blankets on the bed. His real name was Robert Stafford, and he'd been employed in various roles over the years, being a champion wrestler in his younger days, before becoming a Franciscan friar and eventually a member of Robin Hood's infamous gang. More recently, and more relevantly to this business here in Croftun though, he had helped solve the mystery of the 'Christmas Devil'[1] in nearby Brandesburton, and discovered a natural talent for deduction and investigation.

Even so, the tangled web of clues and impenetrable statements from both de Courcys had Tuck at a loss.

---

[1] See *Friar Tuck and the Christmas Devil*

"I really don't know what to make of it," he admitted. "For now, I think all we can do is make sure Lady Isabella is not molested again during the night." He grinned and pulled the blanket up around his chin before Little John could protest. "You can take first watch."

* * *

In the next room Lady Isabella reached out to her husband and he came across, placing an arm around her shoulders as he sat down.

For a time they sat in silence, the injured, traumatised young woman drawing strength from her spouse, who yawned and shook his head tiredly.

"Who do you think is doing all this to me?" Isabella asked softly. "And what do you think they want?"

The nobleman pondered the question for a long moment then sighed. The day's events had left them both drained and he was unable to think clearly.

"I don't know," he admitted, squeezing her shoulder reassuringly. "But we'll find out eventually, and then we'll deal with it once and for all."

"I was so scared today," Isabella said, and he felt her tensing beside him, as if she was preparing to flee from the now-departed attacker. Or fight back.

"I believe you," de Courcy replied. "But you can rest easy tonight, knowing you have those outlaws in the adjoining room." He laughed suddenly and she glanced up at him, confused. "Forgive me," he said. "I just realised how ludicrous that statement sounded."

The lady smiled too then and the fear that had played around her features for the past few hours seemed to leave her expression entirely.

"You're right," she agreed. "But asking a couple of infamous, violent criminals, to keep away another makes a strange kind of sense, doesn't it? Besides," her smile faded and she became serious again, although not downcast. "I get the feeling Brother Tuck and the bailiff are good men, no matter what the old stories say about them."

"Our previous king saw fit to pardon them," de Courcy shrugged, rising to his feet and eyeing her intently. "If Edward thought them trustworthy, I suppose we should too." He lifted her uninjured hand and kissed it, then bid her goodnight and opened the door to call for Anne.

"I love you, Adam," the lady said, but he was already gone, and she lay down once more, praying God would grant her at least a few hours of dreamless sleep.

CHAPTER FIVE

All was quiet during the night, and the next day – once Little John had collected the fine he was there for in the first place – he and Tuck rode back to Wakefield. There was little they could do in the manor house and the snow had mostly melted in the pale sunshine, making little barrier to travelling the five miles or so to town.

Lady Isabella was sad to see them go but John promised to return at a moment's notice should any other incidents occur. Sir Adam was advised by the bailiff to move his wife to a bedchamber on the second floor, with a sturdier bolt on the door. Possibly even purchase a dog for her as a pet.

The nobleman appeared entirely unconvinced by these suggestions, but promised to look into them regardless.

And so the men from Wakefield – both of whom were wealthy thanks to their time with Robin Hood – settled back into their usual routine as the people around them prepared for the coming winter.

Little John had returned to blacksmithing after his time as an outlaw, but he found it boring to be cooped up inside all day following years of living mostly outdoors. So, although he didn't need the wages, he had taken a job as a bailiff again, serving writs, collecting fines, arresting felons and enjoying spending time travelling around the local countryside. The Sheriff of Nottingham and Yorkshire, Sir Henry de Faucumberg, knew John well, and was more than happy to employ the giant warrior once more in this less formal role than most bailiff's were used to.

Friar Tuck lived in Wakefield as well nowadays but was not officially part of the church there, instead passing his days wandering around the surrounding villages, helping people who needed medical or spiritual aid. And, of course, his evenings were usually spent in one of the taverns, enjoying the meat, drink and gossip that folk were always happy to provide him with. His jovial nature and eagerness to help anyone in need meant he had many friends dotted all over the north of England.

Yet, for all that, he was still a formidable man who could more than hold his own in a fight, and his sparkling eyes masked a deep intelligence and wisdom that John and the other members of Robin Hood's band had often found invaluable.

One evening, the pair met in the local alehouse and sat nursing ales and enjoying the warmth from the hearth as an icy rain battered the roof overhead.

The inn-keeper's daughter walked past, carrying drinks for a group at another table. She was about the same age as Lady Isabella and had a similar neat figure and the sight of her reminded John of events at Croftun.

"They make a strange couple, don't you think?" he said, leaning back on his stool and stretching out comfortably. "The de Courcys I mean. He's a fair bit older than her and, well, not quite as attractive." He rolled his eyes and went on before Tuck could answer that. "You know what I mean. As men go, he's not as handsome as she is. I'm just wondering how they got together. He must have money or power, or both, I suppose."

"You're wrong," Tuck replied, crossing his arms over his chest and smiling. "I mentioned them to Father Myrc, and he says their marriage was apparently one of love, rather than something arranged by their parents – Isabella's father didn't even like Sir Adam and wanted her to find a husband closer to her own age."

"Love?" the bailiff looked sceptical. "I mean, aye, they seem comfortable with one another but…Sir Adam doesn't strike me as being particularly passionate about his wife, it has to be said."

"You could be right," the friar said. "Because the money was all on Lady Isabella's side."

"Ah…" John nodded and took a sip of ale, gazing into the hearth thoughtfully. "Well, I'd say he got the best of the bargain."

"Aye," Tuck agreed. "Isabella's father was a wealthy merchant who somehow ended up owning the land around Croftun Manor. She fell in love with Sir Adam and, despite her father's reservations they were wed." He shrugged. "I've seen stranger couples being quite content in their lives over the years. Take you and Amber for example. How a giant, ugly oaf like you managed to snare her I'll never know."

"Me neither," John laughed good-naturedly.

"You know the cook, Reynardine, was also upset by Lady Isabella's wedding," Tuck said thoughtfully. "She told me so herself."

John raised his head, eyes narrowed. "Maybe he's involved in all the trouble then. Maybe he's in love with her or something."

"Perhaps," Tuck replied, and they sat in contemplative silence, oblivious to the alehouse's other patrons all around them.

Eventually, they finished their drinks and returned through the howling winter wind to their homes, mostly forgetting all about the de Courcys and the strange happenings at the manor house.

But then the bailiff came to his old friend one November morning, about a month after their previous visit to Croftun.

"What's the matter?" Tuck asked, seeing the worried expression on his friend's face and putting down the broom he'd been using to clear snow from the chapel pathway.

"Lady Isabella," John replied, and that was all the friar needed to hear.

With a nod, Tuck ran indoors to St Mary's, and returned moments later wearing a heavy cloak and carrying a small pack that was undoubtedly stuffed with provisions. It wasn't far to Croftun, but it made sense to be prepared when making a journey during wintertime. "What's happened now?" he demanded.

"I'll tell you on the way," Little John replied, and led the way to the stables near the centre of the busy village, where his horse stood saddled and ready to ride. A moment later, a young lad led the friar's chestnut mare out, similarly prepared for a journey, and was rewarded with a coin from the bailiff.

As the youngster went back inside the stables, drawing the doors closed behind him, Tuck and John mounted and kicked their horses into a fast walk. Southeast, to Croftun.

"Well?" Tuck demanded. "What's happened to the lady?"

"Attacked again," John said as they passed the edge of the village and were able to push their mounts faster. Still they could not ride at full tilt for the ground was strewn with wet leaves, their brown, orange and yellow hues offering little relief to the bleak countryside around them.

"But she lives?"

"As far as I know," the bailiff nodded, although the gesture was lost within the motions of riding. "Sir Adam sent a message simply reporting that his wife had been injured and requesting that I come at once."

"Damn it," Tuck said, shaking his head angrily. "We should not have left so soon the last time. We should have investigated more. Questioned the servants properly!"

John didn't reply to the friar's words. They both knew there was little to have been gained by further investigation on their previous visit – Tuck was simply upset by the lady's unfortunate plight. This time they would hopefully find more clues, or perhaps even another witness to the attack.

It took less than an hour to reach Croftun, which was a much smaller place than Wakefield. Although there was a sizeable Augustinian priory dedicated to St Oswald about a mile away, the village centre only boasted a few houses, and a couple of workshops. Little farmhouses dotted the mostly flat countryside, with sweetly-scented woodsmoke curling from their chimneys and carrying on the icy wind to the riders as they headed towards the land belonging to the de Courcys.

As they rode through the slate-roofed gatehouse leading to the manor, Tuck looked more closely at the buildings on the estate. Obviously, the manor house itself dominated the grounds, being a stone-built, two-storey structure rather larger than the others around it. Kitchen, bakehouse, granary, dairy and privy were all nearby, in smaller buildings, while the barns and stables were set a little further away and even a round, stone dovecote nestled among some leafless trees to the east.

Tuck took all this in and despaired. So many places for an intruder to hide!

The sound of their horses' drumming hooves alerted the inhabitants to their arrival, and two servants came out from the stables to take their mounts while Sir Adam de Courcy himself met them at the front door of the house, an agitated look on his face.

"Ah, I see you brought Brother Tuck again," said the nobleman as John approached, and the friar couldn't tell whether his presence was met with pleasure or annoyance.

"He sees things I would miss," replied the bailiff, and Sir Adam accepted this with a slight raise of his eyebrows, before turning to lead them inside. They walked directly to the chamber Lady Isabella had been taken to on their earlier visit, glad of the banked fire in the hearth although no refreshments were laid out on the table for their arrival this time, something which clearly irked de Courcy.

"Excuse me, gentlemen," he muttered, shaking his head irritably. "I'll have Anne bring you something to eat and drink."

Before either Tuck or John could protest their host was gone, closing the door at his back, footsteps rapidly fading along the hallway as he went to fetch the tardy serving girl.

"He seems more irritated than fearful or worried," John said to Tuck. "I mean, given what's been happening. If an intruder had come into my house and assaulted my wife, I think I'd be frantic with worry in case they came back."

The bailiff gave a start as the door opened and Reynardine bustled in carrying a platter of meat and cheese.

"Of course Sir Adam is not worried about intruders," the cook said quietly. "He doesn't think there is one, and never has been."

"Then who—?" Tuck demanded, keeping his own voice low to match the servant's.

The reply stunned him.

"The master thinks Lady Isabella is doing it all to herself," said Reynardine, and walked out just as de Courcy returned.

The nobleman grunted a word of thanks to the departing cook and gestured for his guests to sit down, promising them drinks would also be brought shortly.

"Is the lady all right?" Tuck asked, trying to mask the astonishment he felt at the departed cook's statement.

"She's alive, if that's what you mean," de Courcy replied with a slow nod. "Whether she is 'all right', well...Who can say?"

Little John cleared his throat and asked their host to also take a seat. Tuck knew the big man did not like to deal with people when they were above his eye-level. Which was not very often, admittedly.

"I received your message, my lord," said the bailiff. "Can you tell us what's been happening since we were last here a month or so ago?"

"Oh, I can tell you all about it. In fact, I can do better, and show you." Although they'd just sat down, de Courcy got to his feet again and nodded towards the door. "Yes, that's probably the best way to start. Follow me, gentlemen. I hope this will not upset you too much." He looked back at the former outlaws and smiled mirthlessly. "I forget who I'm talking to. I expect you've seen much worse than I'm about to show you, but still...It may be upsetting on some level."

Friar and bailiff shared a puzzled look but shadowed de Courcy along the corridor until they came to a back door and went outside. He strode across the garden, towards a low, brick building which, from the sounds and smell, Tuck knew must be a kennel.

Heading to the side of the structure, de Courcy pulled out a ring of keys that were attached to his trousers by a long chain and opened the weather-beaten old door before pointing to the ground.

Tuck watched the nobleman with great interest as he placed the keys back in his pocket, and then John and the friar peered into the gloomy storage room, both wondering what in God's name they'd been brought there to see.

"Oh." The massive bailiff's grunt was more surprised than anything else. "I wasn't expecting that."

On the floor of the little room lay the bodies of three cats, in various stages of decomposition.

"These poor beasts are connected, in some way, to your wife's plight?" Tuck asked, frowning as he got down on his haunches to inspect the small carcasses.

"The first one, that blue-grey one on the left," de Courcy replied. "That was found, dead – strangled with the leather cord you can still see around its neck – inside my wife's bedchamber, three weeks ago."

"Dear God," John muttered, shaking his head as their host continued.

"The second – in the middle – was found by Isabella, as she took a morning stroll last week. Again, the cord is still on the body."

Tuck stared at the final little corpse on the right. "This one was not strangled."

"Very astute, Brother Tuck," de Courcy noted, dryly. "My wife found its headless body outside her bedroom door three days ago."

"This is an outrage," Little John growled, rising to his full, impressive height, and gazing down at de Courcy who, unsurprisingly, stepped back a pace. "Are you any closer to discovering who's doing all this?"

The nobleman shook his head. "No, not at all. Are you finished your examination?" Tuck looked around at the question and nodded. "Come then, it's cold out here. Let's go back to the front room and warm ourselves as I tell you the rest of it."

"There's more?" John asked incredulously, but de Courcy merely waved a hand over his shoulder, bidding them follow, which they did, glad to be out of the icy wind and away from the pitiful slaughtered cats.

Tuck wondered where exactly Lady Isabella was but de Courcy was clearly not going to be rushed into telling his tale.

"Forgive me," said the nobleman as they came back into the cosy front room with its blazing fire and table laden with refreshments. "I forgot my manners in all this…upheaval. But you can eat and drink your fill now. I see Anne has finally brought the ale along."

"Think nothing of it, Sir Adam," Little John rumbled, filling a cup and taking a long pull from it gratefully. Tuck also helped himself to the ale and lifted some bread and fruit preserve, always happy to fill his belly.

De Courcy seemed to have little appetite however, perhaps as a result of viewing the dead cats again, and he took no bread or ale. Instead, he banked the fire and returned to his favoured position by the window until Little John asked him to continue with his account of recent events at the manor house.

"You are wondering where my wife is," the nobleman stated, and didn't wait for a reply, continuing as he came across to sit in front of his guests. "She is upstairs. In her bedchamber, which is, of course, a different one to where we found her on your last visit." He shook his head and apparently changed his mind about needing a drink, filling a cup from the jug on the table and draining it in one go. "She is injured. Quite badly I fear."

"Same as the previous occasion?" Tuck asked sorrowfully. "No witnesses?"

"None," de Courcy agreed. "No vile notes this time either."

"What happened to her then?"

"We don't know. She is still to recount her tale."

Tuck set down his cup and stared at de Courcy, searching the man's face for some clue to what he was feeling. Fear? Sorrow? Anger? The nobleman was difficult to read however, and the friar decided to ask the question that had been playing on his mind since Reynardine's incredible comment earlier on.

"Is it possible, Sir Adam, that your wife is doing all this to herself?"

De Courcy's eyes narrowed as he met Tuck's gaze, probably wondering what had put this idea into the friar's head. "Yes, I think it is a possibility," he admitted at last. "I do not see how an intruder could steal onto our estate and perpetrate these crimes without anyone noticing them – there are servants in the house and workers in the fields even at this time of year for God's sake. And to leave no clues, apart from the ones they want us to find?" He threw his hands up in the air in exasperation. "Yet today…Saints preserve us, how could someone do *that* to themselves?"

Little John frowned. "Today's attack is worse than last time? I wouldn't have thought it could get much more severe than having a knife shoved through your hand into a floorboard."

"Oh, there's no bloody wounds this time," de Courcy replied. "Another scarf was used to throttle her though, and it pains me to say she is still unconscious." He raised a hand in response to his visitors' cries of alarm. "She is alive, and the surgeon

– who arrived before I sent for you, bailiff, although he's gone now – tells me she should be all right, in time."

"Why do you question whether she did this to herself today then, my lord?" Tuck asked, pursing his lips. "As incredible as it seems, I suppose your wife's present condition could be the result of some self-administered trauma. People have occasionally been known to injure themselves on purpose, for a variety of reasons."

"That may be true, Brother Tuck," de Courcy nodded. "But when we found her this morning, she was lying on the floor unconscious, with her hands and feet tied together *behind her back*!"

CHAPTER SIX

At that moment there was a soft knock on the door and the serving girl, Anne, pushed her head into the room. "Forgive me, Sir Adam," she said. "You asked us to let you know when the lady woke up..."

"At last!" de Courcy exclaimed. "Come, gentlemen. Now that Isabella has regained consciousness we might find out what happened to her down there."

The nobleman hurried from the room without waiting for Tuck or John, who glanced at one another.

"'Down there'?"

Tuck shook his head at his friend's bemused look. Wherever the lady had been found, they would soon know the truth of it.

They hurried up a flight of stairs to the floor above and de Courcy took them to a room in the western corner. Unlike his servant downstairs, he thrust the door open without knocking or otherwise announcing their arrival.

Bailiff and friar were right behind him as he rushed over to the bed and took his wife's hand in his own, but they had to watch their feet as a medium-sized dog skittered past them out of the room, tail between its legs.

"Are you all right?" de Courcy was asking his wife as Tuck watched the white canine disappear down the corridor they'd just walked along. He was a dog lover and, despite the brevity of the situation at the manor house, felt slightly disappointed that he couldn't pet the animal.

"I think so," Lady Isabella said in a rasping voice, smiling weakly at her husband, who, relief now replacing anguish on his face, took a seat beside her on the bed. "What happened to me?"

Little John also sat down, unbidden, knowing his great size could be intimidating whether it was his intention or not, while Tuck closed the door and met the stricken woman's questioning gaze as he replied. "We were rather hoping you might tell us, Lady Isabella."

Her face screwed up and a soft cry broke from her lips as she suddenly touched the red marks on her neck, remembering that part of her ordeal at least.

They waited for her to regain her composure and the friar looked around the chamber approvingly. Set on the upper floor, this was much more suitable for Lady Isabella – no strange night-time visitors would be peering in her window up here and, judging by the rumpled old blanket on the floor, the departed dog kept guard over his mistress while she slept.

Yet it hadn't been enough.

"Take your time, lady," the friar said, folding his hands across his round belly.

"We're in no hurry," John agreed with an encouraging nod of his own which brought a flicker of a smile from Isabella although the haunted look in her eyes remained.

"I will tell you what I can," she started, drawing in a deep breath and wincing as she did so, fingers reaching up to touch her injured neck once more.

"When I awoke this morning Purkoy was not in his bed."

"Purkoy?" John asked, eyebrows drawn together in a childlike expression of bemusement that seemed out of place on his bearded countenance.

"My wife's dog," de Courcy replied. "It passed us on the way in, you must have seen it, bailiff."

"He's very inquisitive," Lady Isabella said. "Hence the name – after the French 'pourquoi.''

"'Why'," Tuck said, and, if anything, John's baffled look only deepened at what he perceived as a terrible lack of manners on his friend's part, questioning Isabella's choice of name for her pet.

The friar, smiling, came to his rescue. "'Pourquoi' means, 'why' in French, John."

"I can see now why you brought the friar with you," de Courcy muttered, rolling his eyes as if John was an idiot and Tuck was proud to see the giant bailiff holding his temper. Back in their outlaw days the nobleman would surely have found himself grabbed by the throat and pinned against the wall for his cutting remark.

"His bed was empty," Isabella said. "And my door was lying open. I assumed one of the servants had come in – perhaps to check on me – and accidentally left it ajar when they left, with Purkoy taking the chance to explore."

"What kind of dog is it?" Tuck asked.

"Is that really relevant?" de Courcy asked.

"I have no idea, my lord," Tuck replied flatly. "I am merely trying to gather all the facts, so we have a better picture of what happened."

"Peace, Adam," Lady Isabella chided her husband, then smiled at Tuck. "Purkoy is a spaniel."

"Not the greatest guard dog in the world," de Courcy grumbled. "I wanted to get a mastiff, a big fierce thing, but Isabella wouldn't have it."

"I don't want a big smelly lump lying around my bedchamber," the lady said tartly. "Purkoy is a companion as well as a watchdog."

"You dressed and, I assume, went to find the hound?" Tuck asked, to stop the couple's inane bickering as much as to drive Isabella's narrative along.

"That's right," she agreed. "I called for him, and checked the rooms on this floor of the house but there was no sign of him and the servants could not say where he might be. So, I went downstairs." Her face clouded over again and a small shudder wracked her body.

De Courcy touched her arm reassuringly and muttered soft words of encouragement that seemed to bolster her for she returned to her tale soon enough.

"I could not find him on the ground floor either, and there was hardly anyone around. Only Anne was working in the hall, but she hadn't seen Purkoy, so I left her to her sewing and continued my search."

"Is it usual for there to be so few people around at that time of day?" Tuck asked, looking from Isabella to her husband.

"It's not *un*-usual," de Courcy replied with a shrug. "We don't retain a huge number of servants, and I expect they were all busy in the kitchen or in the grounds. I don't think there's anything sinister in it, honestly."

Tuck nodded, eyeing Isabella for any clues to her own thoughts on the matter but her apprehensive expression gave little away.

"I was going to go up to my chamber and fetch a cloak," she went on. "So I could continue my search outside. But then I noticed the door to the undercroft was open."

"*That* was unusual," Little John said, noting de Courcy's pursed lips at this piece of information.

"Yes," the nobleman admitted. "The undercroft is usually kept locked with a key hidden nearby for Reynardine if he needs access. I have fine imported wines stored down there and I do not want the servants helping themselves to it."

"'Fine imported wines'," the lady repeated sardonically. "That's an understatement."

"They are very expensive?" Tuck asked.

"We are not paupers," de Courcy said stiffly, and his eyes silently admonished his wife for her words. This was an old point of contention between them, the friar guessed. "I enjoy a nice cup of wine in the evening after a hard day's work. Speaking of which…"

Without another word, the nobleman rose from his wife's bed and strode to the chamber door, bawling down the corridor. "Anne!"

Moments later the sound of footsteps could be heard running up the stairs and then the red-faced serving girl appeared.

"Yes, Sir Adam?"

"Bring us—" He broke off, glanced back with a frown and then said, "A jug of ale and cups." He dismissed her with a gesture and she hurried off to fulfil the master's command.

Tuck and John exchanged amused looks. De Courcy had been about to call for some of the fine expensive wine he was apparently craving, and then, realising he'd have to share it with his guests, decided ale would suffice instead.

Lady Isabella appeared irritated and no wonder, having her traumatic story halted while her husband called for drinks.

The de Courcys' relationship seemed strange to Tuck, but he had known many married couples over the years – he'd occasionally been the one performing the wedding ceremony, after all. Lots of them, most perhaps, had their own little ways that seemed very odd to outsiders. From what he'd seen though, Sir Adam and Lady Isabella cared for one another well enough, despite the obvious tensions between them.

And, although it was the lady suffering the assaults, the whole situation must be stressful for both. Perhaps it was understandable that the nobleman needed a drink.

Soon enough, Anne returned, and cups of ale were set out for the four people before the servant retreated downstairs once more with a look of relief on her face.

Lady Isabella did have a few sips of the ale, which the friar took as a good sign, before she returned to her tale. Her husband paced the room, checking the lock on the window and stroking his chin as he listened.

"As I said, the door to the undercroft was ajar, which I thought a little strange since only my husband

and Reynardine have keys. But, obviously, we keep food stored down there. There's nothing Purkoy enjoys more than a piece of cheese! So, I located a candle, lit it from the fire in the front room, and went downstairs."

"You went alone?" Little John asked. "Forgive me, my lady. After recent events, I'm surprised you would have the courage to go down into a dark cellar on your own." He smiled to offset his words. "I certainly wouldn't."

"Perhaps it was foolish," she admitted. "But I felt no sense of danger – I was more worried about where Purkoy had gone than thinking of any threat to myself. Besides, it wasn't any darker down there than it is anywhere in the rest of the house every winter's night when the fire's gone out, and I refuse to allow my tormentor to frighten me into changing my ways."

The bailiff nodded. Her point about the darkness was fair enough, and he admired her fortitude, but he still thought her actions peculiar, given everything that had happened in the past year or two.

"At the top of the stairs I called for the dog," the lady continued, "and I thought I could hear him. But he didn't come to me, so I went down, holding the candle aloft. I must admit, the further I went, the more nervous I became. But I was *sure* I could hear Purkoy now – whining pitifully, as if in pain or fright. That bolstered my courage and I went on." She stopped and took another drink then glanced around at the three men. "It might seem strange to you – I've only had the dog for a few weeks, but we've become good friends in that time."

Tuck shook his head with a knowing look. "Not strange at all, lady. A spaniel can be as good a friend as any, and better than some."

His words made her smile and she carried on with her account. "I could see Purkoy's white coat by the back wall, so I started walking towards him, speaking softly because I could tell he was upset." She trailed off, and stared at the floor, a look of anguish on her face. "His muzzle had been tied shut so he couldn't bark, just whimper. And he was so frightened he'd made a mess all around himself. I could see it on his coat." She began to cry at the memory of her beloved dog's plight, and the three men remained silent, waiting for her to find the strength to go on.

De Courcy walked over with the jug of ale and refilled her cup. She took a sip, hand shaking so violently that her husband had to help her bring it to her mouth without spilling the lot. He set it back down on the low table next to her and she drew in a deep breath.

"And then," she said, very quietly. "My candle went out."

CHAPTER SEVEN

"Someone pressed against my back and put...something...around my neck. They pulled it tight, strangling me so hard that I couldn't breathe. He was strong, and pulled me right down to the ground..." She had stopped shaking by now, and a new emotion filled her eyes: anger. "I tried to fight him off but...The way he had me pinned, I couldn't get any leverage into my blows, and then I started to pass out."

"Did he say anything?" John asked, head cocked on one side almost like the departed spaniel. "Was there *anything* to give you a clue who he was?"

She nodded slowly, but took a moment to reply, gathering her thoughts so she reported her tormentor's words accurately, although her anger had dissipated, replaced once more with an anxiety that was horrible to behold. "He said if I told anyone who he was he would kill my dog and my family."

Sir Adam de Courcy jerked upwards at this, fury in his demeanour. "Oh, he did, did he? Well..." He patted the hilt of the sword he was wearing at his waist – a new, and understandable addition to his usual attire. "If the bastard comes after me, he'll find himself dead soon enough!"

Little John raised a hand, exhorting the angry man to calm down and not add to his wife's upset.

"Did you know who he was then?" Tuck asked, and he thought she hesitated for just a moment, but then shook her head, crying silently again at the terrifying memory.

"Is that all you can remember, lady?" John asked in a soft, reassuring voice.

Isabella nodded and lay back on the bed, drained by her emotional tale. "I'm sorry. I wish I could tell you more, but I didn't recognise his voice."

"What about a scent? Did he have a distinctive smell?"

The lady once again paused for a moment before addressing John's question, as if about to impart some new information but, as before, simply shook her head. "All I could smell was poor Purkoy's mess and my own sickly sweat."

"Damn him!" John muttered. "We have nothing to go on whatsoever."

"I'm so sorry," Lady Isabella repeated, but John shook his head and assured her it was not her fault.

"Whoever this man is, he's clever. Knows his business, as despicable as it is."

"We'll find him though," Tuck said. "Rest easy, Lady Isabella – we will investigate this attack more thoroughly than we did the last one." He glanced at John, half-expecting a frown of disapproval in reply, but the giant bailiff was nodding grimly.

The woman's plight had affected him as much as it had the friar. Maybe even more, Tuck thought, for Little John had always despised men who offered violence to women. Indeed, dealing with such a man had been the reason John was declared an outlaw – a wolf's head – years before. If they ever did catch whoever was doing all this to Lady Isabella, Tuck feared the bailiff would mete out his own brand of justice before the law could follow its proper course…

"I hope we do find him," de Courcy growled, gazing into the gently crackling fire. "I've had enough of all this."

Friar and bailiff shared a look. The man might well love his wife, but he seemed to care more for his own feelings, even at a time like this. The result of a pampered childhood Tuck guessed – certainly, Sir Adam was not the first noble he'd come across with a narcissistic streak and would surely not be the last.

"Where's the rope that was used to bind your wife, my lord?"

De Courcy's head jerked up at John's question, for he'd been lost in thought and it took him a moment to register the bailiff's words.

"Still in the undercroft," he said eventually. "When I noticed the door was open I suspected something bad had happened, so called for Reynardine to accompany me. We went down together and found Isabella." He shook his head at the memory. "I wasn't about to carry her back up here bound hand and foot, so we cut the ropes and left them there. Reynardine helped me bring Isabella up the stairs."

"Who took care of Purkoy?" Isabella asked.

De Courcy made a face, as if the dog's fate meant nothing to him. "I assume Reynardine went back down and cleaned the hound up, or sent someone else. I didn't take much notice of it – I was more concerned with you, my dear."

There was silence in the room then. The day's disturbing, frightening events were all out in the open now and everyone did their best to take it all in. It seemed impossible to make sense of it, Tuck thought, but he vowed to do everything he could to make sure Lady Isabella didn't have to endure another ordeal such as the one just described.

"May we go down to the undercroft and examine the area?" the friar asked, and de Courcy instantly perked up.

"Of course, I'll take you there myself, I—"

"No," Tuck broke in. He smiled, but his tone was firm and left little room for argument. "You should remain here to look after your wife. Someone must guard her after what's happened today and that surely has to be your mission, Sir Adam."

"He's right, my lord," John said. "I'll go down with the friar and see if there's any clues to be found."

"May we take Reynardine with us as a guide?" Tuck asked and de Courcy nodded irritably. Clearly, he didn't really like the prospect of sitting in his wife's chamber for the rest of the day but didn't want to argue and appear anything other than the diligent, protective spouse.

"All right," Little John said, opening the door and ducking to pass through. "We'll return soon and let you know if we find anything. You rest, Lady Isabella, and fear nothing – your husband will take care of any more intruders that seek to disturb your peace."

Tuck followed his massive friend out into the corridor, closing the door behind them and raising a finger to his lips to warn John not to say anything about their host's rudeness, or the fact the lady appeared to be hiding something from them.

They made their way down the stairs but, before they could find the serving girl, de Courcy's voice filled the air calling her name and they shared a knowing look.

"I wonder if he'll share his expensive wine with his wife," John muttered, shaking his head in amused disgust.

"Don't be too hard on him," Tuck laughed. "Put yourself in his shoes. Would you share your best imported wine with us?"

"If I was a nobleman, Tuck, I wouldn't give you the steam off my morning turd," Little John smiled, clapping the friar on the back. "But Sir Adam is still an arrogant prick."

"God forgive you," Tuck replied, making the sign of the cross as Anne ran past them to discover what the master wanted her for.

"That must be the door to the undercroft." John leaned along the hallway leading to the rear entrance and roared even louder than de Courcy had done moments before. "Reynardine!"

"You're learning how to be a nobleman yourself, I see," Tuck noted sardonically, raising an eyebrow.

The bailiff shrugged and gestured towards the back door as it was thrown open and the cook bustled in, a somewhat fearful look on his face. "Easier than going hunting for him, wouldn't you agree?"

"Who called?" Reynardine demanded, his fear evaporating as he saw the smiling bailiff and suspected he was the butt of some joke. "I have work to do you know."

"We need to talk to you about what happened to Lady Isabella," Tuck said, before John could say anything. "Fetch us some candles, if you would, my friend, and take us down into the undercroft where you found her. Don't worry, Sir Adam knows about it. He's taking care of the lady in her chamber, and Anne is fetching her dog, Purkoy."

As he spoke, the sound of claws scrabbling on the stone floor came to them, growing louder until the white spaniel appeared from the room to the left, apparently responding to Tuck's mention of his name.

"Hello, boy," the friar said, smiling and leaning down to stroke the dog's soft, long ears, pleased to see its tail wagging and seemingly quite over the traumatic ordeal it had suffered just a few hours before. It moved from Tuck to John and then to Reynardine, teeth pulled back in what could only be described as a smile as it enjoyed their attention, and then, perhaps realising they had no food, it wandered back into the room it had come from and was out of their sight.

"He seems happy enough," John said, and Reynardine, frowning, nodded agreement.

"Aye, he does. But he was shaking like a leaf when we found the lady earlier. Poor little bastard had shit all over his coat, and he was pressed against the wall as if he wanted to disappear right into the stone." He shook his head and looked towards the room the dog had gone into. "Whoever, or whatever, frightened a dog like that, and did what he did to the lady, well…" He met Little John's gaze, although he had to crane his neck to do so. "I pray to god you find the devil soon, bailiff. Someone like that needs locked up, or, even better – strung up on the nearest tree!"

The cook followed Purkoy into the side room and returned moments later carrying three long candles. He handed one each to friar and bailiff, keeping one for himself, then reached up, standing on tiptoes, and searched with his fingers along the top of the undercroft doorframe.

"Here it is," John said, easily plucking the key from its hiding place which was no hiding place at all to one as tall as him. "Here you go."

Reynardine took it, smiling and shaking his head at the bailiff's prodigious size, and Tuck knew this day would not be forgotten in a hurry by the old fellow. Little John was a legendary figure to everyone in the north of England – as was the friar himself – and it was highly likely that this journey down to the undercroft would form part of some exaggerated tale told in alehouses all around Yorkshire and Nottingham in the coming months.

Tuck prayed the story would have a happy ending…

"Lead on then, friend," John commanded and Reynardine, unhappily, opened the door and, bracing himself against whatever evils might yet lurk in the dark cellar, began walking down the stairs.

The bailiff followed with Tuck bringing up the rear, all three peering into the shadows nervously. It was one thing to face a known, human opponent with sword or quarterstaff – quite another to take on the supernatural forces that made the blackest places of Earth their home…

The hairs on the back of Tuck's neck stood on end and he muttered a soft *Pater Noster* but his voice only seemed to make the gloom more foreboding and he trailed off, choosing instead to rely on his trusty cudgel which he took out from its hiding place beneath his grey robe.

"You check that corner, Tuck," Little John said, gesturing with the long knife which he'd drawn soundlessly, their candle flames flickering from its bright steel. "I'll go this way. Reynardine, just you wait here in the centre, in case anyone is still here and tries to escape."

"All right for you to say," the cook grumbled, eyes wide in the dim light. "I don't have a weapon though, apart from my little eating knife."

It was highly unlikely the man who'd attacked Lady Isabella would still be hiding down here, for he'd surely know the place would be searched. But they had to make sure – it wouldn't be the first time a felon had returned to the scene of his crime for some reason.

"Nothing here," John reported, using his candle to inspect every nook and cranny of the western side of the undercroft. "Tuck?"

"Same," the friar said, voice echoing from the stone walls. "Just us, and a lot of wine and food."

"Always thinking about your stomach." The bailiff laughed as they returned to a relieved-looking Reynardine in the middle of the large room.

"You wouldn't be thinking about eating if you'd been here earlier," the cook grumbled, and Tuck shoved his cudgel back into his belt and patted the man on the arm apologetically.

"I'm sorry, Reynardine," he said. "It must have been a most unpleasant experience for you. Take no notice of our humour, it's the result of many months and years living as outlaws in the forest where, if you can't laugh, you might as well just give up all hope."

The cook nodded, mollified, and pointed to the back wall. "Over there is where the dog was lying. His mess is still there – someone will have to clean it up I suppose, but no-one wants to come down here unless they need to right now."

John walked across to the spot, face screwing up as the overpowering stench hit him, but he leaned down, lighting the filthy ground with the candle, noting the rope that must have held the frightened Purkoy in place. The other end was wedged beneath a barrel.

"Clearly this was setup in advance," Tuck said. "As bait, to lead Lady Isabella into the trap."

"Where did you find her?" John asked, and the cook lifted his candle aloft to illuminate more of the room, eyes scanning the ground until he saw what he was looking for and led the way just a few feet to the side.

"There." He pointed, and they saw more rope discarded on the ground. "Hands tied behind her back. Feet too. Like I say," he held up his eating knife again. "This is the only weapon I usually have with me. Thankfully it was sharp enough to cut through the ropes."

Tuck peered at the ropes and Reynardine's knife whose blade was keen enough, no doubt, but it must have taken a while to get through the sturdy bindings.

"Sir Adam didn't have anything more suitable with him?"

Obviously, a sword would have been too unwieldy for such a delicate task, but, with everything that had been going on in the manor recently, the friar would have expected the nobleman to have a dagger of his own.

"Not that I know of, Brother Tuck," replied the cook.

No matter – de Courcy must think his sword was enough to deal with any attackers. The man, as far as the friar knew, wasn't an expert in hand-to-hand combat the way he and Little John were. The fact that a sword was a pretty useless weapon indoors, thanks to ceilings and walls and furniture getting in the way of its long blade, apparently hadn't occurred to the nobleman.

John handed his candle to Reynardine and got down on his haunches. He lifted the ropes, testing their strength and examining the knots. "Very crude," he said as Tuck knelt beside him. "Whoever did this was no sailor."

"Effective enough," the friar noted.

"Aye. Look how long they are though. Seems a bit much, don't you think?"

"I'm not sure," Tuck said, cocking an eyebrow at his friend. "How much rope do you normally use to tie up your victims?"

"You know what I mean," the bailiff retorted, shaking his head with a smile. "I know the ropes did their job, but they seem long to me. There would have been room to wriggle about, to work them loose and escape."

Tuck shrugged, staring at the bindings. "Well, we know the attacker isn't trying to kill Lady Isabella."

"What?" Reynardine cried, candles sending shadows flickering around the chamber as he jerked upright indignantly. "If you'd seen her—"

"She's still alive," Tuck broke in, then went on in a softer voice, more suited to the gloomy atmosphere. "She has now survived at least two attacks where the intruder has had her completely at his mercy. If he truly wanted her dead, she would be."

John got to his feet, still holding the ropes in one hand while retrieving his candle from Reynardine with the other. "What's it all about?" he muttered, shaking his head and looking around the dark chamber for some hidden clue. "Why would someone go to all this trouble just to frighten Lady Isabella?"

"Maybe it's some vindictive person she upset years ago," Tuck suggested. "A former servant, let go for some misdemeanour perhaps. Or a childhood sweetheart who took rejection hard. Or…it could just be a madman."

Reynardine nodded agreement. "Whoever it is, they're certainly mad. No sane man could do this to the lady. She's the kindest mistress any of us have ever known."

Tuck was surprised by this statement and he stared at the cook in the darkness, trying to tell if the man was sincere or not. The flickering candles offered no clue however.

John let out a long sigh. "I suppose so. Some men do enjoy inflicting pain and fear on others for no good reason. Philip Groves for example."

Tuck suppressed a shiver as they headed for the stairs, remembering the sadistic killer they'd faced alongside Robin Hood just three years earlier.[2] Groves and his gang had murdered many people, even children, in his insane quest to bring down

---

[2] See *Blood of the Wolf*

Robin and his friends. He was a good reminder of just how depraved, and irrational, men could be.

And yet, as they gladly left the darkness of the undercroft behind them, Tuck couldn't help thinking about those ropes they'd found, and John's comment about their length. They *did* seem rather long for the purpose ascribed to them.

Long enough for Lady Isabella to have tied *herself* up?

It was possible. He'd seen prisoners escape from their bindings in the past by contorting themselves into strange, unnatural positions, although he had never heard of someone tying their own hands and feet behind their back.

It seemed too incredible to be true, but Tuck knew it wasn't only men that acted unpredictably at times – some women did too, of course.

Even sweet, smiling noblewomen.

CHAPTER EIGHT

"What will you do?" Sir Adam de Courcy looked tired. His face was drawn and there were bags beneath his eyes that hadn't been there just a few weeks before. "What *can* you do?" The anger that had been an integral part of his countenance during recent conversations also seemed to have gone, replaced, perhaps, by desperation.

He had taken Tuck into the main hall to discuss their findings in the undercroft. The dog, Purkoy, had returned to his mistress's bedside and she seemed quite content with the arrangements. Brave woman, Tuck thought – many would have asked for someone to guard them while they recovered from such a heinous attack. And again, there was that niggling voice that suggested she could afford to be courageous if she knew there was nothing to fear…

"I think we," Little John gestured towards the friar, "should stay here for at least a couple of days." He held up a hand before de Courcy could comment, in agreement or otherwise. "Hear me out, my lord. I suggest me and Tuck ride off, as if returning to Wakefield. We'll then return here when the sun goes down and stand guard, secretly, over your wife."

"Not a bad idea," the friar nodded. "If all remains quiet, nothing has been lost other than a little of our time. On the other hand, we might catch the perpetrator in the act, and save Lady Isabella from another, possibly even more vicious, assault."

De Courcy regarded them both and Tuck could almost hear his thoughts: *Or maybe they'll find out my wife is doing all this herself and we can all move on in the knowledge she's mad!*

The nobleman didn't say the words out loud though, he simply nodded and admitted John's plan was the most sensible one. "I'll have Reynardine keep watch for your return tonight. Come to the back door, at the kitchen, and he'll let you in."

"You're sure of his loyalty then?"

"Oh yes, bailiff," de Courcy nodded vigorously. "The man thinks the world of my wife. All the servants do, as far as I know. He was just as upset as I was when we found Isabella in the undercroft this morning."

"What about the girl?" Tuck said. "Anne. She'll need to be told we're here or she'll get the fright of her life if she happens to see us lurking about the house in the darkness."

"I'll tell her," de Courcy agreed. "And I'll order her not to say a word to my wife about your presence."

Little John glanced at Tuck, who nodded. One way or another they had to clear this matter up, no matter how it turned out. If Lady Isabella was the architect of the whole elaborate scheme, she needed help before it went too far.

They clasped forearms with the nobleman and went to the stables to fetch their horses. The young lad there had taken good care of the animals, brushing them down and feeding them, so John tossed him a small coin in thanks.

"Did you see any strangers around the grounds today?" the bailiff asked as he hauled himself into the saddle.

The boy, no more than fourteen years old judging by his hairless chin, shook his head. "No, sir."

"Well, keep your eyes open," John said. "If you see anyone, or anything, that seems out of place, let us know. We'll be back in a few days, and you'll be well rewarded for any information."

Grinning at the prospect of a few extra coins, the lad promised to stay vigilant and waved as the two Wakefield men cantered off towards the town.

It was a pleasant, cloudless afternoon, although the low sun made them squint as they rode and they knew the coming night would be a frosty one. After a mile or so they reined in their horses and led them off the path into the trees. Both men knew this whole area well from their years as outlaws and they soon found a clearing to rest and wait for night to fall.

De Courcy had told Reynardine of their intention to return and keep watch over the manor house and he'd also commanded the cook to make them up a small pack of provisions to share until sunset. They dismounted and found fallen logs to sit on while they tucked into the bread, cheese, salted pork and ale.

"Do you really think the lady is doing all this to herself?" John wondered, flicking a crumb of cheese from his cloak.

Tuck shrugged and shook his head slowly. "Who knows? I think it's possible, and there's some evidence to suggest it's true. I certainly believe she knows more than she's telling us." He washed down a piece of meat with a draught of ale and asked the bailiff for his thoughts.

"I think it's someone from outside," John said. "Someone we know nothing about. The lady doesn't seem like a lunatic to me and, although he's a bit arrogant and self-centred, Sir Adam appears genuinely anxious about the whole thing."

Tuck had to agree with both of those assessments and yet the idea of an outsider committing the attacks was rather far-fetched, for surely someone would have seen an intruder stalking the estate.

And if it was Reynardine behind it all, well, it was quite clever of him to tell them Sir Adam believed his wife was harming herself. That hastily muttered statement from the cook had confused the whole thing.

"Do you think it's odd that they don't share a bedchamber?" John asked, breaking into his thoughts, but Tuck shook his head.

"Not at all. Nobles often sleep in separate rooms. Perhaps Sir Adam snores – or even the lady! It's also more hygienic and, well, who knows how they came to be married? They may like one another well enough but perhaps they have no desire to be intimate."

The bailiff grunted. "It's a different life to what I'm used to, that's for sure. Us poor folk live in draughty little houses with only one or two rooms and have to huddle together in bed for warmth during weather like this."

"You're not poor anymore," Tuck laughed, popping another slice of pork into his mouth. "We all made our fortune with Robin. You could afford a manor house like the one in Croftun if you wanted."

"Aye, maybe so," John admitted thoughtfully, then he winked and grinned suggestively. "But I like sleeping next to my wife, and she doesn't mind my snoring."

They sat eating their meal in companionable silence for a time, going over the day's events in their minds, trying to make sense of it all.

"One other thing," said the friar at last, tossing a small piece of bread onto a pile of sodden brown leaves for the robin that was darting around their feet hopefully. "When Lady Isabella was telling us what happened to her in the undercroft, you asked her if she'd noticed anything about her attacker. In particular, you asked about smells."

"I did," John replied, also watching the red-breasted bird as it chased off an interloper encroaching on its territory. "So?"

"Her eyes flickered away from your face for just a moment," Tuck recalled. "Maybe it was nothing, but I wondered if perhaps she *had* noticed something that she didn't want to tell us."

"Like what? Surely she'd want the bastard caught more than anyone. Why would she hide any information from us?"

Tuck had to admit he wasn't sure. Perhaps she suspected one of the servants but didn't want to get them into trouble without being absolutely certain of their guilt. Such an accusation – from a noblewoman, against a lowly servant – would be quite devastating, legally, to the person it was directed towards.

"Well, hopefully our mystery-man makes an appearance tonight," John growled, locking his fingers together and stretching out his arms. "I'm looking forward to seeing how he deals with someone bigger than himself."

"If he even exists," Tuck said and the two of them stretched out beneath their thick travel cloaks to catch a little sleep in preparation for the night ahead.

At last, the sun began to dip beneath the horizon and they woke up, remounted and headed back to Croftun Manor before it became too dark to travel safely.

They tied their horses to some trees near the gatehouse and went the rest of the way on foot. As arranged, Reynardine was watching for them and he let them in the rear door, promising he'd take their mounts to the stable for the night.

The pair had decided beforehand where they'd spend the next few hours, with Tuck heading upstairs to the small room opposite Lady Isabella's chamber, with an extra blanket and a small cup of unwatered wine to take the chill off since he couldn't have a fire in the hearth without giving away his presence. From that room though, if anyone came along the corridor, he would hear, or see, them.

Little John, similarly outfitted, positioned himself in the room directly beneath the lady's, on the ground floor, where he could watch for anyone approaching the slumbering noblewoman's window.

Hours passed and nothing happened. The house remained silent until dawn approached and, frustrated, the two hidden guardsmen met up and slipped away to the kitchen where they ate breakfast and caught up on some sleep.

It had been a long, bitterly cold and boring night and the investigation was no further forward.

But they followed the same routine the next night, and the next after that.

"We're getting nowhere with this," John grumbled on the fourth morning as they ate Reynardine's porridge. "We could keep watch for the rest of eternity and not see anything."

"I suppose so," Tuck said, blowing on the bowl of hot milky oats. "We might as well head home. You'll be looking forward to seeing Amber."

The bailiff's eyes lit up at the mention of his wife. "Aye, it'll be nice to sleep in a proper bed with her again. Sir Adam might like spending his nights alone, but I'm fed up with it."

"So, we are still no closer to solving the mystery," said a cold voice and they turned to see de Courcy standing, stony-faced in the doorway. From his demeanour, they guessed he'd heard John's comment.

"I'm afraid not, my lord," Tuck said, rising to his feet respectfully and gesturing surreptitiously for his companion to follow suit. For his part, John appeared unconcerned about offending their host. In fact, his eyes twinkled mischievously, and the friar almost laughed himself. The giant bailiff had never been one to care about upsetting noblemen.

"Sit," de Courcy muttered, striding over to take a place at the small table beside them and they resumed their meal. "I suppose we just wait until the next time something happens to Isabella then."

There wasn't much to say to that statement. It was both depressing and true.

They finished the porridge and de Courcy promised to send a messenger if he had need of them again, and then they left, riding hard through the winter countryside for Wakefield.

CHAPTER NINE

Tuck feared they would be called upon by Sir Adam de Courcy in a few weeks perhaps, but he was shocked when, the very next morning, the stable boy from Croftun Manor rode into Wakefield asking for the bailiff and the friar.

"Surely nothing's happened?" John said throwing his clothes on as Tuck appeared at his home. Apparently the bailiff had been making the most of his own comfy bed and his wife's companionship, for it was unlike the bailiff not to be up and about at this time of day. "We spent three bloody nights freezing our bollocks off in that house, and nothing happened. Yet the minute we leave, there's another attack?"

"I'm afraid so, sir," the stable hand replied, smiling shyly at Amber, who handed him a small cup of ale to refresh himself after his ride. "Well, not exactly. Lady Isabella is quite safe and well." He sipped his drink and looked away as John pulled on his trousers, quite unaware he was revealing everything to all in the room.

"In the name of God," his wife chided, laughing. "You're not living in the greenwood anymore, John. Cover yourself up – the friar doesn't want to see your hairy arse at this time of the day."

"The friar's seen my arse more times than you know," John grinned, winking at the stable boy who gaped back, shocked. "It's hard to find privacy when you live as an outlaw in the forest with a dozen other men."

"Unfortunately, that is true," Tuck admitted ruefully, before turning seriously to the young messenger. "What's happened then, lad? Let's have it. You say the lady is alright?"

"Aye," the boy confirmed. "But she woke the whole house up last night, screaming. She says someone was outside. They threw a pine cone, or an acorn or something at her window to wake her up then…well, they said things to her. Sir Adam can tell you what – I don't know myself, but it shook her up pretty badly, so Anne says."

"Oh, that's just bloody typical," John said angrily. "I sat watching for anyone coming to that window for three nights, freezing my balls off, more bored than I've ever been in my life, and what happened? Nothing. Yet the minute we leave, the bastard turns up at that very spot!"

Tuck shared his friend's disappointment. It seemed very convenient that Lady Isabella's mystery tormentor stayed away the whole time they were on guard, yet struck again as soon as they left. Almost as if he – or she – knew their movements.

"Come on then," John grumbled, kissing Amber and gratefully taking a piece of buttered bread from her. "We'd best go and see what's been happening. I need to collect another fine from the same man as the last time anyway, so I'd have had to visit the estate sooner or later. Lead on, lad."

The three of them headed to the stables and soon were riding hard for Croftun once more.

"Seems more than a coincidence that this happened the very night after we left," John said, letting the stable boy ride a little way ahead so he wouldn't hear their words over the pounding hooves of the horses.

Tuck nodded. "Agreed. But if you're suggesting Lady Isabella has fabricated the story, just remember: She didn't even know we were on guard the previous three nights."

John frowned. "Maybe not. But Reynardine did. So did Sir Adam, and Anne. And all three knew we had gone home yesterday morning..."

They rode the rest of the way in silence and Sir Adam was waiting to receive them as they thundered up to the house. He waited until they'd dismounted and his stable boy had taken their horses away before greeting them.

"The lad told us your wife is safe, my lord," Tuck stated, and the nobleman nodded as he ushered them into the house and led them to the now familiar hall on the ground floor.

"Isabella is fine," de Courcy said as he closed the door behind them and gestured to the seats by the fire. They gladly sat down and thrust cold, red, wind-cracked hands towards the welcoming flames gladly, waiting for him to continue. "But it's the same old story," he muttered, shaking his head and, as seemed to be his habit, walked over to gaze out the window onto the gardens. "She says this fellow woke her up and said terrible, hateful things to her. But…"

The room fell silent other than the crackling fire for long moments, until John said, "But?"

De Courcy turned and moved to join them by the hearth, warming his own hands before it just as they'd done. "But there's no other witnesses. As usual."

Tuck had grown tired of avoiding the issue and decided it was time to come out and demand to know de Courcy's true thoughts.

"You believe Lady Isabella is making this whole thing up, don't you?" he said, making sure to keep his tone neutral.

"I do!" The nobleman cried in exasperation. "Don't you?" He took a seat beside them and went on in a softer, calmer voice. "All the evidence suggests so. As you might imagine, as soon as it was light enough, I checked the ground beneath my wife's window. It had been a freezing, cloudless night, yet there wasn't a single footprint in the frost."

John blew out a long breath and nodded at their host. "That is suggestive, obviously."

"Suggestive?" De Courcy gave a sardonic laugh. "It *proves* no-one was outside Isabella's chamber! Unless they were some kind of demon who floated along without having to stand on the grass." He sighed and held his head in his hands as if at the end of his tether. "She is mad. It's the only possible solution. I've long suspected it, but now…I can't see any other explanation."

"Is it not strange that this latest incident occurred on the very night after we'd left?" Tuck said. "After all – your wife did not know we were standing guard over her. So why would she make this up on the very day we were no longer there, watching for intruders?"

Little John turned to see de Courcy's reaction to this pertinent question, but the nobleman's anger flared up again as he replied.

"We can thank that stupid bitch Anne for that. She told Isabella yesterday that you two had been here standing watch but had given up and gone home." He thumped a hand angrily on the arm of the high-backed chair and shook his head furiously. "I ordered her to keep her mouth shut but, well, you know what women are like."

"But why?" Tuck demanded, shaking his head in confusion. "What possible reason could Lady Isabella have for subjecting herself to these torments?"

"A man of your experience," de Courcy replied dryly, "must have heard of similar cases in the past. People who seem to have more than one person inhabiting their body. Or a demon perhaps. Most times, such unfortunates don't even realise it's happening."

Tuck narrowed his eyes thoughtfully. It was true – he had personal experience of such people, but before he could say anything, the nobleman went on.

"Or it could just be she craves attention, like a naughty child. They care not whether they are punished or rewarded – they simply desire to be noticed. And..." He looked down at his hands and toyed with the wedding ring on his finger, seeming reluctant to say any more. With a resigned breath, though, he lifted his gaze back to meet the friar's. "Isabella's father once told me that she had been just such a child. She would demand his attention and, if he took no notice, she'd go off and start fires. Fires! She once burned down a barn before the servants could bring the blaze under control!" He forced a smile onto his face. "At least she grew out of that, eh? Blessings for small mercies."

"I think we've heard, and seen enough," John said sorrowfully into the silence that followed de Courcy's statement. "It seems like there's no other explanation. As hard as it must be for you to admit, Sir Adam, I can only agree with you: Lady Isabella is doing all this to herself. This latest event, and the lack of footprints to show the presence of an intruder, is enough for me to say so. I'm sorry, it must be a bitter draught to swallow."

The nobleman heaved a great sigh, as if his world was collapsing around him, but he raised his eyebrows and tried to appear hopeful. "At least we can move on from this, and stop hunting a non-existent, shadowy tormentor. How I'm going to help Isabella, well, I don't know…" He looked at Tuck and there was a humility the friar hadn't seen before. "You're a man of God. Should I pray for her? Is she possessed?"

"I wouldn't like to say that, Sir Adam," Tuck replied cautiously. "I've seen people in the throes of demonic possession before. Remember Holmfirth, John? The whole place – everyone living there – went mad, thanks to the dark influence of one individual. But," he finished, as the bailiff nodded hearty agreement, "I've not seen any evidence that Lady Isabella is acting in a similar, bizarre manner. If she *is* possessed by a devil, it is hiding itself well."

"What do you suggest then?"

"Well, my lord, it might be helpful if I talk to her alone." De Courcy narrowed his eyes but Tuck forged on. "Sometimes those under the influence of a demon know it's happening, but are frightened to admit it, especially to those close to them. She might never speak about it to you, her husband, but perhaps she'll open up to a stranger. I am, as you point out yourself, a man of God."

"He has a way of coaxing secrets from people," John said, nodding at de Courcy reassuringly. "Oh, not by force or threats – he just has an easy way about him. I think it's the pudgy face and slightly simple expression he wears most of the time."

Tuck threw his friend a black look, and his eyes widened when he noticed de Courcy hadn't realised the bailiff's words were a joke.

"Yes, I suppose it might work," the nobleman finally assented. "All right, Brother Tuck. She is in the same chamber as before – we couldn't keep moving her around the place every time anything happened. Go to her, and ask why she's been doing all this to herself." He came across and placed a hand on Tuck's arm, even managing a half smile. "Tell her we know the truth now, and that you will help her cast out the demons haunting her."

"Very well," Tuck said, rising and heading for the door. "I will return here when I've spoken with the lady."

"And I," Little John said, somewhat apologetically turning to their host. "Have another task to complete while I'm here, my lord. I'm afraid your labourer is late paying another fine. I was going to give him another week or two, for it's only a small amount but, since I'm here anyway…If you don't mind, I will collect it from him now."

"By Christ," de Courcy grumbled. "I'll need to have a word with that fool. His antics will give me, as his master, a bad name."

Tuck ascended the stairs to Lady Isabella's chamber as the voices of John and Sir Adam de Courcy faded behind him. He rapped gently on the sturdy door and lifted the hasp as someone bid him enter.

The lady was in bed, again – it seemed to be her default position these days – and her faithful maidservant, Anne, sat on a chair beside her, sewing. At his approach, the dog, Purkoy ambled towards him, tail wagging, and collapsed on the rug at his feet, gazing up at him, tummy bared for a rub. Tuck laughed at the hound's friendliness and leaned down to stroke the soft white fur.

"He certainly seems to be over the unpleasant experience of a few days ago."

"I think he's too silly to remember it," Lady Isabella smiled, and gestured to the other chair near her bed. "Sit, brother. It's always a pleasure to see you. Anne, please pour our visitor a drink."

Tuck waited until his cup was filled and then looked pointedly at Isabella who, stared back for a long moment before finally understanding his meaning.

"Anne, you may go about some of your other duties. The friar will keep me company for a while. Thank you."

They waited until the door had closed behind the servant and the sound of her footsteps told them she was on the ground floor before Tuck pulled his chair closer to the bed and eyed the young noblewoman intently.

"Why are you staring at me like that?" she asked, puzzled rather than angered by his inspection. Little

John was probably more correct than Tuck wanted to admit – his rather pudgy, pleasant face *did* put people at their ease. It also made them underestimate him, but that wasn't important now. He planned on being quite honest with the anguished lady.

"I am searching your countenance for any signs of madness," he told her. "Or demonic possession."

"Ah." A light flickered in her eyes which Tuck was surprised to realise was born of amusement, instead of the anger he'd expected. "Do you see anything?"

"No," he replied bluntly. "Do you feel mad?"

The lightness in her expression dropped away instantly and she beckoned Purkoy to jump up on the bed next to her. She stroked the animal's long ears and replied in a soft voice.

"Sometimes, yes. But not in the way you mean. Just…all these things that have happened to me. I know my husband suspects me – I can see it in his eyes at times. But I'm not making it up, or doing it to myself – it's really happening. But the stress, the fear…I sometimes feel like I can't deal with it and I *will* go mad."

"Lady, my friend, the bailiff, has come to the conclusion – along with your husband – that you are possessed. They think you are behind the whole thing." He watched her reaction and felt terribly sorry for her as tears welled in her eyes. "If it's worth anything," he said, patting her uninjured hand with a consoling smile. "I believe you, for you bear no marks of demonic possession as far as I can tell. And I plan on finding the person who really is tormenting you."

She looked directly at him and saw the strength in his gaze. Friar Tuck might appear to be a portly, tonsured, jovial man of God, but he was not someone to take lightly.

"What can I do to help?" she asked.

"Well," he said, and his tone became grim. Deadly serious. "There's some things that don't quite add up in all this. I need answers from you, Lady Isabella, and I want the truth. Then we'll see what can be done."

CHAPTER TEN

Tuck left the lady's chamber with a lot to think about. She had been completely open and truthful with him, as far as he could tell, but he still felt like something was missing. A piece of the puzzle that might unlock the whole mystery and give them the answers they needed.

He went down the stairs and found Anne sewing in one of the rooms. He bade her return to Isabella's chamber and keep the lady company which he was happy to do, then he went out to find Little John. There was nothing left to accomplish in Croftun that day, but he had something he wanted to do elsewhere.

He met the bailiff, walking alone back towards the house from the low buildings located in the northern section of the grounds.

"Where's Sir Adam?" the friar asked." Did you collect the fine you went to collect from his labourer?"

"Aye," John said, nodding grimly. "But the daft bastard tried to argue about paying it. Got right up into my face."

"Ah," Tuck smiled. "I expect that didn't go too well for him."

"I put him on his arse," the bailiff admitted, returning his friend's grin. "It ended there though. De Courcy stepped in and had a word with him before it got any more heated."

"'Heated'?" Tuck laughed, gesturing towards the stables. "I expect the poor man would have been unconscious before you even broke sweat. Come on, I have an errand to run and I'd like to do it as quickly as possible."

"Where are we going now?" John asked. "To see some bishop or other, who can cast out the devil inside Lady Isabella?"

"Something like that," Tuck agreed, taking the reins of his horse from the stable hand and clambering into the saddle with more finesse than usual for a man of his size and age.

John followed suit rather more clumsily and, with a wave of farewell, they kicked their heels in, riding back towards the main road.

"Well? Where are we going?" John asked again when they'd passed the Croftun Manor gatehouse and were heading west again. "To St Edmond's Priory? It's in the other direction. There must be someone there that can help you exorcise a demon."

"No, first, we're heading back home to Wakefield," Tuck said. "You can take care of your usual bailiff work for the next couple of days – I have to go to Nottingham, and then on to York."

Little John's smile grew broad as he thought of that. "Good stuff," he cried. "I'm getting tired of this weird mystery and it looks like my part in it is done. You go off to the archbishop or whoever it is you need see in York for spiritual advice, and I'll stand you a drink or two in the alehouse when you've cast out the lady's demon. I don't envy you, old friend – she's clearly got something nasty inside her, and I prefer facing enemies I can see."

"I'll gladly take your ale," Tuck replied, but his expression wasn't as contented as the bailiff's. "This problem isn't over yet though, and neither, I think, is your part in it."

And, much to John's irritation, that was all he'd say on the matter all the way back to Wakefield.

* * *

The priest in charge of the probate records shook his head sorrowfully and spread his hands wide as he looked smugly at the friar. "I'm sorry, but I can't just let you go down and nose about in our archives. You need special permission."

Tuck smiled and brought forth a sealed letter from his grey robes. "I trust this will be enough, friend."

The archivist eyed Tuck suspiciously as he took the proffered letter and looked at the seal. He didn't recognise it, but pursed his lips and opened out the parchment, reading carefully the words written there. "I authorise…my representative…Robert Stafford…and so on and so on. This is from the Sheriff of Nottingham and Yorkshire, Sir Henry de Faucumberg."

Still the man wore a look of uncertainty, almost as if he thought the friar was trying to trick him. Members of different religious orders could be notoriously tribal, and often frowned on one another, as if they were in competition somehow.

"It is," Tuck confirmed. "I rode all the way to Nottingham Castle to get it, wasting two days that could have been much better spent searching for what I need in your records, but I had a feeling someone like you would stand in my way."

"Robert Stafford," the man muttered, eyebrows drawing together thoughtfully. "Where have I heard that name before? Ah, I know – Friar Tuck! You're that fellow that fraternizes with outlaws, aren't you? You give us all a bad name—"

"My fist will be fraternizing with your face in a moment, unless you shut up and show me those records."

"All right, all right, keep your tonsure on." The priest came around to the front of the desk, eyeing Tuck warily, and locked the front door before heading back, through another that led along a high-ceilinged corridor.

Although the main cathedral building in York was hugely impressive, a true monument to the greatness of God, the associated administration structures such as this one were bland and functional. Tuck had seen hundreds of such buildings and he barely registered this one as he was shown to a flight of steps with a sturdy locked door at the bottom. The archivist pulled out a ring of keys, found the correct one straight away and opened the door.

It was pitch black inside for, being underground, there were no windows, and Tuck felt a momentary shiver as the sight and fusty smell of the place brought back memories of the ill-omened undercroft beneath Croftun Manor.

"I'll be back shortly," said his guide, who hurried back up the stairs and disappeared, muttering about his memory going as he got older. The friar sat down on the bottom step, clasped his hands together, and prayed that he would find what he hoped for within the probate records. He had a good idea what lay behind Lady Isabella's recent troubles, but needed confirmation before he would be in a position to help her.

Of course, what he sought here in York might very well prove the opposite of what he expected, and that would point towards Sir Adam and Little John being right about the woman being the architect of her own torments…

The sound of sandals slapping against the stone floor above brought him back to reality and he mouthed a silent "Amen" and crossed himself before getting back to his feet. The archivist appeared, carrying a lit taper, its acrid smell filling the enclosed space as he bustled into the record vault. A moment later a weak orange glow bloomed into life, then another from further inside the chamber, and then another and another before, at last, the priest returned to Tuck's side and extinguished the taper, placing it onto the floor and looking at the friar.

"What exactly are you wanting to see?"

Tuck told him, heart sinking as he gazed around at the huge room which was stacked with what must have been thousands of records. "I really hope you have a system for where things are kept, or we'll be down here until doomsday."

"Of course we do," the priest retorted, personally insulted by the suggestion the record keepers were too stupid to do their job properly.

"Sorry, friend, I was merely making a – rather poor, I admit – jest," Tuck said, and as it so often did, his open face and infectious smile mollified the priest.

"Right, well, you're after this section," the man said, gesturing with an arm. "If you know the year your record was lodged, by whom, and in what parish, that will all help us narrow things down to a specific area."

Tuck gave him what little information he had and, amazingly, within just a few moments the priest pulled out exactly what he was looking for.

"I'll leave you to it then," said the man, smiling proudly at this proof of his skilful organisation. "I have to go back upstairs and open up again. If you would replace that scroll *exactly* where it came from, then blow out the candles so the place doesn't burn down, I would be grateful."

There was a desk and chair handily placed in the room and Tuck sat down to read through his prize as the priest disappeared back up the stairs. It was only a short text, and he was well versed in the Latin it was written in, but the handwriting was rather difficult to make out.

Carefully, he brought out ink, pen, and paper from his robe, and began deciphering the document, praying that his journey here had not been a wasted one.

CHAPTER ELEVEN

Little John grinned at the sight of his friend coming into the alehouse in Wakefield, and called to the barman for another mug of ale.

"Pull up a stool, Tuck," he said. "And have a drink with me."

The friar gladly sat down at the table, stretching out his legs and wincing. He wasn't used to riding long distances around the country and his backside and thighs were aching. A long pull of the freshly poured ale soon brought a smile to his lips though, as did the smell of beef and vegetable pottage bubbling in a pot over the hearth.

"Hungry as ever, eh? Barkeep, we'll have a couple of bowls of your pottage as well, lad." He turned back to the friar. "I've already had some – it's good."

"Does Amber not feed you enough?" Tuck asked, peering at John's midriff critically.

"Aye, but a man of my prodigious strength needs to eat more than most. Besides," he drew in his belly and looked down his nose at Tuck. "I could eat a dozen bowls of pottage every day for a month and still not be as portly as you."

"Portly!" The friar grinned at John's unusually diplomatic choice of adjective and then set to as the shaven-headed barman brought the bowls of food to the table. It was steaming hot, but that didn't stop either man from shovelling it into their mouths greedily.

"Any more word from Croftun?" Tuck mumbled, without even looking up from his meal.

"No," John replied, pulling a piece of gristle from between his teeth before continuing to eat. "Thank God. Maybe now that we know the lady's secret she'll stop harming herself. How did you get on in York anyway? Did you speak to the archbishop or something? About casting out the demon?" He laughed suddenly. "I remember you and Father Myrc trying to exorcise the mad villagers in Holmfirth, what a day that was. Remember that crazy old hag lifting her skirts and telling you to fu—"

"I remember it all too well," Tuck broke in, shaking his head sadly. "And yes, my trip to York was successful. I got what I needed, and, in the morning we'll ride one last time to Croftun Manor to put an end to this."

"Sounds good," the bailiff said, scooping the last drop of gravy from his bowl.

"In the meantime, I will have a few drinks with you, and pray to God for blessed relief from the pain in my backside!"

* * *

The next day was bitterly cold and Little John was less enthused about their trip to the manor house than he'd been the night before in the cosy alehouse. Tuck was firm though, and, soon enough, the pair were well wrapped up in thick cloaks, their horses' hooves pounding along the frosty road to Croftun.

This time when they arrived no one was waiting to greet them, but the sound of their approach brought the stable boy out, eager as always to take care of the horses.

"Is your master at home?"

"He was, Brother Tuck," the boy replied. "But I saw him going out just a short while ago. Over there, towards the stream. I think he must have been going to make a temporary repair on one of the fences."

"Really?"

"Aye, bailiff," the boy said, taking hold of John's horse's bridle. "The fence down that way has been needing a couple of replacement spars on it ever since the last storm."

"Your master was carrying wood and tools for the job?"

"No," the stable hand replied, shaking his head at such a ludicrous suggestion. "But he was carrying a length of rope, and that's good enough for a temporary fix."

They left him and knocked on the front door of the house. It was opened by one of the male servants who let them inside where the girl, Anne, noticed them. She put down the sock she was darning and came over to wish them a good morning.

"Is the Lady Isabella in her chamber?" John asked, but the servant shook her head.

"No, bailiff. She took Purkoy for a walk a while ago."

"Alone?" Tuck demanded. "After everything that's happened to her?"

"She's a very…confident woman, my mistress," Anne replied tactfully. "She refuses to live in fear. Besides, she has the dog – he'll look after her."

"He didn't the last time," Tuck growled, and both Anne and Little John frowned at his harsh tone.

"What's wrong," the bailiff asked, following Tuck as he headed for the stairs leading to Isabella's bedchamber. "Why are you so irritable this morning?"

The serving girl was at their back and, halfway up the steps the friar stopped dead, causing them all to almost bump into one another.

"Anne," he said, "why did you tell Lady Isabella that we'd been keeping watch over her for those three nights recently? You were specifically ordered *not* to say anything to her about it."

The worried look fell from the girl's face to be replaced by one of righteous indignation.

"I did not tell her you were here, Brother Tuck. I never breathed a word to her, or anyone else, other than Reynardine."

"Come, girl," John said, shaking his head. "We know you told her. Sir Adam was pretty pissed off by your loose tongue."

"Well, bailiff," retorted Anne, quite red-faced now. "As God is my witness, I never told the lady about you being here. I don't know why Sir Adam blamed me for something I didn't do."

John searched her face for some sign that she was lying, but her anger was real and he eventually decided that she was telling the truth.

"Come on," Tuck commanded, moving up towards Isabella's chamber again. "Anne is not to blame for any of this." He knocked on the door and, receiving no reply, opened it.

"I told you, she took the dog for a walk—"

Anne fell silent as Purkoy walked across from his bed, tail swishing from side to side, and nuzzled against Tuck's leg. He was the room's only occupant.

"What the hell is going on, Tuck?" John demanded, sensing now that something was wrong and realising his friend knew more about it than he was letting on. "Where is she?"

"Did your lady tell you where she planned to go?" the friar demanded, ignoring the bailiff's question.

Anne nodded. "To the stream. She likes it there on a cold day like this, says it's nice and peaceful and helps her clear her mind."

"Oh shit," Tuck burst out, uncharacteristically. "Come on, John, we have to hurry!"

The friar thundered down the stairs and along the hallway towards the back door, which he threw open seemingly without care for anyone that might be on the other side. The bailiff raced after him, muttering darkly to himself about this strange and wholly unexpected turn of events.

He hadn't seen Tuck run this fast in years.

The frost-rimed grass didn't slow them up as they sprinted towards the narrow stream that snaked through Croftun's grounds although John's massive stride and better physical condition brought him level with his friend soon enough.

"Are you going to tell me what the hell is going on?" he demanded. "What's this mad dash all about?"

"You wanted me to exorcise a demon, didn't you?" the friar cried, almost losing his footing before righting himself and pointing towards the narrow, dark line bisecting the land. "Well that's exactly what we're going to do. Look!"

"By all that's holy—" Little John surged ahead, thundering across the frozen ground as he finally caught sight of Lady Isabella. "Get your hands off her you bastard!"

Hearing his warning cry, Sir Adam de Courcy looked up, anger flushing his face. He stopped what he was doing though, and glanced all around, as if checking to see if more men were converging on him. Seeing no-one, he let go of the rope he was tying around his prone wife's arms, and sprinted away, following the course of the stream.

"Get him, John," Tuck shouted, now past the limit of his endurance and breathing heavily. "I'll take care of Isabella. If de Courcy hasn't already done away with her, the freezing ground will soon kill her."

"Come back here, you smug little prick!" John roared, needing no encouragement to go after the fleeing nobleman and, as he raced away Tuck quickly reached Lady Isabella's side. Kneeling, he took out his knife and sawed carefully through the bonds around her wrists, which her attacker had, as before, bound behind her back.

They'd come upon him before he could finish tying her legs, but she was not moving and her face was deathly pale, her lips already a terrible shade of blue.

As on previous occasions, a scarf was wound tightly around the lady's neck, making her pass out or, God forbid, expire completely, and Tuck gently loosened it, marvelling at the strength he had to use on the task for he was loath to use the dagger so close to her face.

"Almighty Father," he prayed, shaking his head in anger as he cradled Lady Isabella against him, trying desperately to restore warmth to her cold, flaccid limbs. "Let her be all right. And let John catch the scum who did this!"

CHAPTER TWELVE

Little John was still a fit man, his great bulk being mostly muscle rather than fat, and he soon began to gain on the fleeing nobleman who was, apparently, running with no real destination in mind. There was nowhere to hide out here in the open and the realisation must have dawned on de Courcy that he had only one chance to escape his predicament.

Stopping, he turned to face the pursuing bailiff and, rather to John's surprise, drew the sword at his waist, spinning it around deftly in his hand. Expertly.

The bailiff had faced many men in battle over the years and, although the sight of de Courcy setting his feet in a defensive stance made him wary, a vengeful grin tugged at the corners of John's mouth.

"You think you can kill me, like you were going to do to your wife, eh?"

De Courcy nodded but appeared calm and barely out of breath despite his run. "I do. I was the best swordsman in my company back in my army days and, although you have a greater reach, I feel my speed and agility will give me the edge."

John's only reply was an amused grunt. He'd heard similar boasts before, but few men had ever managed to get the better of him in a fight. Even when he was an outlaw, and the members of his gang would spar, only a select few could match him.

Still, it was quite possible that Sir Adam de Courcy could use a longsword as well as Robin Hood himself, and John was experienced enough not to be over-confident. He drew his own blade and walked slowly towards the nobleman, whose calm demeanour – despite being caught in the act of trying to murder his own wife, and now facing down a giant, legendary warrior – was oddly chilling.

"So it was you all along?"

De Courcy struck out, aiming the tip of his sword at John's belly, but the bailiff parried it easily enough and the pair moved around, widdershins, gazing into one another's eyes, searching for any hint of their opponent's next move.

"I'm no fool," the nobleman replied coolly. "If you want to know the true story of Isabella's troubles, maybe Saint Peter will tell you all about it at the Gates of Heaven." He lunged forward again, but stopped his thrust when it was only half-completed and tossed his sword over from his right to his left hand.

It was a fluidly executed and daring move which might have thrown another opponent completely off balance. The bailiff had seen such tricks in the past though and, before de Courcy could strike, John stepped forward a pace and lashed out with his foot.

De Courcy's eyes widened in surprise but he managed, somehow, to move his knee before the great boot could crash against it and both men stepped back, swords drawn up once more, staring murderously at one another.

"Tuck already knows what you've been up to," John growled. "Even if you manage to kill me," he feinted towards the noble, mainly to force the man back rather than with any real expectation of landing a killing blow, "your days are numbered. You'll hang for your crimes."

De Courcy leaned to the side, looking past John at the figures still huddled on the grass by the stream. John could almost see the gears spinning in the nobleman's head, wondering if he could kill John before heading back to deal with the friar as well.

"You can forget that idea," the bailiff grinned. "Even if you manage to beat me, Tuck isn't the fat, bumbling oaf you think he is. He's a better fighter than most, and as ruthless as any when it comes to dealing out God's justice."

"I'd better cut you down quickly then," de Courcy said, and came on once more, swinging his sword in a shallow arc, forcing his opponent to parry, again, and again. "As soon as I've dealt with you, I'll just make for the stables and ride for the docks. Shouldn't be too hard to find a ship out of the country."

His chattering, a sign of his arrogance perhaps, made him less focused than he should have been when facing an adversary as skilled, and strong, as Little John. As de Courcy launched another attack John parried the blade with incredible force, rather than simply batting it aside as he'd been doing until then. The swords came together with a thunderous clatter and de Courcy cried out in pain as the terrible, unexpected shock lanced along his arm and he lost hold of his weapon.

It fell on the grass and the nobleman clenched his wrist, grimacing, but before he could gather his wits John was upon him, hammering a knee into de Courcy's midriff and dropping him onto the ground, winded. As the would-be murderer tried to stand up again, John leaned down and punched him savagely in the mouth.

There was no getting up from such a blow, and Sir Adam de Courcy simply lay there, curled into a ball, making a strange keening sound that suggested to the bailiff that he'd smashed at least a couple of the bastard's front teeth. John grinned wickedly, then sheathed his blade and bent to search his enemy for concealed weapons.

He found only a short dagger, but its keen blade would be enough to make sure the beaten nobleman wouldn't cause any more trouble. "Get up, de Courcy," he commanded, stooping again, this time to lift the man's dropped sword before tossing it far away, across the stream.

"I said, 'get up'!" he repeated, grasping the nobleman by the front of his tunic and hauling him onto his feet. De Courcy attempted to lash out, but his blow was weak, and John cuffed him hard around the ear. "Any more of that and I'll use your own knife to cut your heart out, you hear me?" John pressed his bearded face against de Courcy's and finally the reality of his defeat seemed to master the noble. His shoulders slumped and he started to walk back towards Tuck and Lady Isabella, still clenching and unclenching his right fist to try and alleviate the pain there.

"Is she dead?"

Tuck glanced up at de Courcy as they approached, disgust on his usually jovial face, but it was the bailiff he spoke to. "Take off his cloak, John – the lady needs it more than he does. We must get her back indoors to the warmth as quickly as possible if she's to survive."

"You heard him," John spat, hauling at the nobleman's thick woollen cloak. De Courcy struggled instinctively but another brutal slap about the head made him more pliable and soon enough Tuck was wrapping the lady with the garment.

The rope that had been used to bind her still lay on the grass and John lifted it, using his confiscated knife to cut away some knots, leaving him with a straight piece which he used to bind the unresisting Sir Adam's hands behind his back.

"Come on," the friar grunted at last, gently lifting Isabella in his arms as if she was a child and setting off at a fair pace towards the manor house. John shoved his captive after them, almost sending him sprawling onto the frozen ground as they silently followed Tuck.

"My lord?" Reynardine must have spotted their approach for he stood at the back door, gazing at the strange party as they returned to the house. "Are you all right? What's the meaning of this, bailiff?" This last was directed in a surprised tone towards John but Tuck broke in imperiously.

"Never mind that, you fool. Bank the fire in the front room and have Anne warm some wine, quickly! There'll be time for explanations once the lady is safe and comfortable."

Reynardine glanced at his unconscious mistress, then once again to his sullen master. De Courcy's eyes flickered to his captor, perhaps contemplating asking his servant for aid, but the memory of John's giant hand slapping him across the ear kept his mouth shut and the cook bolted inside without another word.

"Do you want me to take a turn carrying the lady?" John asked, seeing Tuck breathing heavily, but the friar shook his head a little irritably at his friend.

"Thanks for asking, although it might have been better if you'd asked *before* we were at the house and I'd done all the hard work."

They went inside and headed straight for the room at the front of the house where Tuck and John had first met with Sir Adam de Courcy and learned about this whole sad affair.

Reynardine had carried out his orders and a good fire was burning in the hearth although there was no sign of him now as the friar lay his burden down on the couch. The cook appeared moments later however, carrying a jug filled with wine and another of ale and, at his back, came Anne with a thick blanket.

The serving girl's face was ashen as she took in the sight of her mistress and her eyes grew wide as she saw Sir Adam bound and obviously held captive by the huge bailiff. She knew her place however, and helped Friar Tuck wrap Isabella in the blanket, before sticking a poker into the fire as Reynardine hurried off to fetch mugs.

No-one said a word while the iron heated, and the cook came back carrying an armful of empty mugs, some of which he filled with wine, the rest with ale. Then Anne took the poker out from the coals, tip glowing red, and plunged it into the nearest mug of wine.

The liquid fizzled as a sweet, wonderfully inviting smell filled the room, and Tuck lifted the cup and held it to Lady Isabella's lips. For a moment there was no movement and everyone in the room looked on in trepidation, wondering if she had finally succumbed for good to her attacker's violence.

At last, her mouth twitched and parted slightly as the friar tipped a small amount of the warm liquid in. The lady squinted, but swallowed a little, so Tuck gave her another sip. This time she choked, and her eyes fluttered open, but the colour was slowly returning to her face and the watching audience, with the exception of Sir Adam perhaps, seemed to relax.

She was alive, for now at least.

"What…" Her voice was a mere croak, but then her eyes fell on her husband standing next to Little John and a look of anguish contorted her features.

Tuck grasped her hand firmly and placed his face in front of hers.

"You have nothing to fear now, lady," he said. "You are perfectly safe. And he," the friar threw a disgusted glance over his shoulder at the so-called nobleman, "will harm you no more."

"The bastard will find himself swinging from a rope if I have my way," Little John growled, leaning down to glare at de Courcy who, unexpectedly, laughed.

"You think I'll hang? Really, bailiff?" He shook his head condescendingly. "For what crime? I haven't killed anyone, have I? Or stolen anything. I assume you and the fat friar are accusing me of assaulting Isabella but…" He raised his eyebrows and smirked at the bailiff. "Even if I *did* attack her – is that a crime? A hanging offence?"

Little John stared at de Courcy murderously but the room was silent as everyone gathered there took in his words and understood the truth of them.

Certainly, there would be some punishment from the law for what the man had done to his wife, but it would be a simple fine. No incarceration, no hanging, not even a turn in the stocks on market day.

"Why?" Lady Isabella finally asked. "I thought we cared for one another."

The nobleman looked sorrowful for the first time that day. "I am sorry, Isabella. I do care for you but…" His voice trailed off, the desire to explain his actions outweighed by the knowledge that further words would merely incriminate himself. "I am sorry."

"Sorry?" the lady cried and although she could only manage a hoarse gasp the venom in her eyes spoke volumes. "You're sorry are you? For torturing me all these long months? For stabbing a knife through my hand? For strangling me? For abusing poor Purkoy?" Her expression turned hard and her voice became like ice. "You disgust me."

Anger flared in de Courcy's face and Little John took the opportunity to slap him again. When the nobleman made as if to fight back despite his hands being bound, John grabbed him by the neck and slammed him against the door which thumped in its frame so hard the entire house shook.

"Go on you little bastard," the bailiff growled. "Give me an excuse to show you how we used to deal out justice in the greenwood."

"Leave him!" Lady Isabella gasped and all eyes turned back to her. "Please. Let him talk, if he will. I must know his reasons for doing this to me."

"He's not going to talk," John said. "Are you? Maybe I could beat a confession out of you."

"There'll be no need for that," Friar Tuck said, placing a hand on his friend's arm. "Let him be. I will explain everything as best I can."

CHAPTER THIRTEEN

De Courcy laughed derisively. "You know nothing, you fat oaf."

"On the contrary," Tuck countered. "I know everything. Including your motives for acting as you have."

"Oh, shut up," Isabella hissed at her husband before he could insult the friar again. "Please, Brother Tuck – go on. I get the impression you've suspected Adam all along."

Before continuing Tuck glanced at Reynardine and Anne who were still in the room, apparently too intrigued by events to go about their duties as they should. Lady Isabella took his meaning but simply shrugged in response.

"Let the servants hear," she said. "They should know what kind of master – or should that be monster – they have. But first, please?" Gesturing to Anne she bade the girl refill her wine mug, and that of everyone else apart from Sir Adam who rolled his eyes at the slight.

Reynardine once again poked the fire into life, for it had started to snow outside again and the cold seemed to seep into the very fabric of the building. Then, when everyone had a fresh drink, Tuck sat down on one of the chairs with a tired sigh and began his tale.

"To answer your previous question," he said to Isabella. "No, I didn't suspect your husband from the beginning. At one point I even suspected Reynardine."

The cook protested loudly at this, and Isabella shook her head in surprise.

"Why would you think that?" she said. "Reynardine has been a faithful servant to me for my entire life."

Tuck shrugged. "After that first attack you told me Reynardine had been upset with you since the day you were married."

"Only because I didn't want her to wed that horrible bastard!" the cook spat, pointing at his disgraced master.

Tuck smiled. "I know that now, my friend, but at first you seemed a more likely suspect than Sir Adam. He appeared to me as attentive as most husbands are to their wives and, although he's arrogant and conceited, so are many noblemen. In my experience at least."

"You seem to forget the door to her chamber was bolted from the inside when Isabella was attacked that first day you were here," de Courcy said. "Clearly that suggests my wife must have harmed herself. I was not in the room with her when it happened – unless you think I can walk through doors and walls."

"I admit, that threw me off at first," Tuck admitted. "And later, when other things happened, I did begin to wonder if the lady was indeed the cause of all the strange events. But!" He held up a hand and half-smiled at Isabella. "We know for certain now that your husband was the perpetrator. We caught him in the act of trying to murder you after all. So, I will tell you everything that put me onto his trail and, ultimately, allowed us to stop him just in time."

"I'm looking forward to this," John said, sitting down on a nearby stool but keeping a watchful eye on their captive the whole time. "I still don't see what tipped you off."

"First – let's think about that door to the lady's chamber." Tuck walked across to stand beside de Courcy. "How could someone have assaulted Lady Isabella, and then escaped from within the room when it was bolted from the inside? Well, if you examine the frame around the door you will see there is a gap of about this much," he held up thumb and forefinger. "Just enough for someone to attach something to the bolt inside, and then pull it over from *outside the room*. But what could be used for the task? Well, how about a key chain like that one?" He pointed to Sir Adam's waist, where his keys hung, as they always did.

"That's ridiculous," the nobleman sneered but Tuck shook his head firmly.

"It is entirely possible," he stated. "And I can prove it later if need be, for I've done it myself. So much for the bolted door." He sat down again and addressed Isabella. "Then we spoke to you when you'd revived, and one thing you told us stuck out to me. If you remember that first conversation we had, you said the person attacked you from behind and applied, "pressure pulling me down," I believe were your words."

Isabella shuddered at the memory and nodded uncertainly. "That's correct. But what—"

"Let me give you a demonstration, my lady." Tuck gestured for Little John to come over and stand behind him. "You are tall for a woman, Lady Isabella – just a little shorter than me I'd say. Now, John, put your arm around my neck and act as if you were trying to choke me."

"Act?" John muttered, leaning down and smiling before turning serious again at the irritated look in Tuck's eyes. "Like this?"

The bailiff did as he was told and, as the friar's heels lifted off the floor it was quite apparent to everyone that the pressure being applied to him was raising him up, not down.

"You see?"

Isabella nodded as John returned to his seat by de Courcy. "Whoever attacked me was smaller in height."

"Exactly," Tuck confirmed and again everyone stared at Sir Adam de Courcy who was half-a-head shorter than his wife. "He's only a little fellow, although strong enough, as you found out to your cost, my lady."

"Why don't you go and drink some more communion wine, you fat fool?" De Courcy's face was red with indignation at this entire affair but his words made Tuck tilt his head, almost like a dog who'd just heard something interesting.

"While we're on the subject of wine," the friar said. "Remember that 'expensive wine' Sir Adam didn't want to share with us, John? Well, that will come into things later. For now, just bear in mind that imported wine costs a lot of money."

"What has this to do with anything?" de Courcy shouted, making Anne wince. "So I like good wine, what of it?."

Tuck narrowed his eyes at the angry noble. "Like I say, we'll get to that in time. For now, we're still on the subject of that first attack. You," he pointed at de Courcy, "told us that there had been threatening notes sent to your wife many times over the past two years."

"And?"

"You never thought to hold onto any of them. They would have been important clues."

"I told you – Isabella was upset by them, so we destroyed them all."

The lady shook her head, a bemused frown on her youthful face. "I never wanted them destroyed. I wanted to show them to someone. No wonder you wanted them burned – they were written by you!" She shook her head and laughed sadly. "What a fool I've been."

"Moving on to the next event," Tuck said. "The dead cats. Three cats brutally killed and left about the manor for Lady Isabella to find. Yet no strangers were ever seen in the grounds? That seems too improbable."

"Not impossible though," de Courcy said with a smirk and the friar nodded.

"Granted. But, along with everything else I'd say it points towards someone within the house being responsible."

"Aye," the nobleman cried, pointing at his beleaguered spouse. "My moon-touched wife!"

"The next time we were called here," Tuck went on, ignoring the outburst. "Was when the lady was assaulted and found in the undercroft. She wasn't the only one to suffer that time – the dog, Purkoy was also traumatised. Think back to that day, John, when we went into the lady's chamber. Do you remember the dog?"

The bailiff frowned and stroked his unruly beard thoughtfully. "Not really. I recall seeing it downstairs after that. We were petting it."

"Right," Tuck agreed triumphantly. "When we went into the lady's chamber with Sir Adam, the dog ran straight out with its tail between its legs. Terrified. Yet, when we were downstairs – just me, you and Reynardine – Purkoy came out to see us and appeared perfectly happy. What can we infer from that?"

"You bastard," Isabella spat, hatred now twisting her features as she glowered at her husband who regarded her impassively. "How could you frighten my dog so badly? And then tie him up like that, in a pool of his own shit and piss? I wondered if it was your voice that day, but I refused to believe it. It was simply too incredible to accept!"

Tuck let her rail at de Courcy for a while, feeling it would do her good to get some of the pent-up frustration and fear out of her system but when she trailed off, voice a tired croak, he addressed her again.

"Why did you go down into the undercroft, my lady?"

"Because I couldn't find Purkoy and was afraid something bad had happened to him."

"Yet you went down there, in the dark, all alone, despite everything that's happened to you over these past months and years."

She stared at him as if he was mad. "Of course. I love Purkoy. Wouldn't anyone do the same for their beloved pet?"

Tuck smiled and turned again to de Courcy.

"And what did *you* do when you noticed the undercroft door open and suspected your wife might be in trouble down there? You called for Reynardine to come with you to investigate."

De Courcy shrugged. "Only a fool would go blindly into danger alone."

Tuck shook his head in disgust. "You supposedly feared for your wife's safety, yet, rather than going immediately to her aid as any other man in this room would have done," he looked to John and Reynardine and received terse nods in response, "you stood there and waited for someone to come with you. Why? Because you needed a witness, that's why! You knew if you were to find the lady all by yourself suspicion might fall upon you."

"Maybe he's just a coward," Little John suggested and the disdain in his eyes clearly stung the captured nobleman. "The lady was brave enough to go into the dark, scary cellar all alone, but not you, eh? You needed someone to hold your hand. Pfft." The bailiff laughed scornfully but the target of his ire remained silent for once.

Lady Isabella sipped her warm drink and said, "When you questioned me that day, Brother Tuck, you asked if I'd smelled anything when I was being attacked. I didn't want to tell you at the time, because, well, I simply couldn't bring myself to believe it but...There was a faint, if distinct, scent, of that wine Adam loves so much. I told myself I was imagining it, that my senses were just playing tricks on me. But things are making sense now..."

De Courcy hooted with laughter and looked from Anne to Reynardine, as if trying to win them over now that he knew the others were dead set against him. "She's just making things up now. There was no mention of this so-called smell at the time."

Neither servant replied although the uncertainty in their expressions had faded since Tuck had begun laying out the facts as he saw them.

"Me and John decided to spend a few nights here, keeping watch in secret over Lady Isabella," the friar carried on with his narrative, refusing to be sidetracked by de Courcy's protestations. "Sure enough, when someone was actively watching for intruders, nothing happened. Yet the very day after we left, someone threw pine cones at her window to wake her up, then stood outside calling obscenities to her."

"No-one did anything of the sort," de Courcy growled. "I told you I looked all around the frosty grass beneath her window."

"Yes, you searched the grass," the friar nodded, before turning to the old servant. "Reynardine, did you look also?"

The cook glanced at his master as if seeking permission to speak, then decided he didn't need it after all. "I did," he confirmed. "Later on. There was only one set of footprints, as he says."

Tuck nodded. "So the only footprints left there were yours, Sir Adam. Not because the intruder was a lie, however. No, it was because *you* were the man muttering that filth during the night, weren't you?"

"You had me convinced," Little John said to the guilty nobleman. "All that bluster about killing whoever was tormenting the lady. You even told Tuck to go up and tell her we knew she was possessed by a devil!"

"This is all a pointless waste of time," de Courcy said. "Your tale is a mad work of fiction, *Brother*, and none of it can be proved. Anne, pour me a cup of wine, girl, I'm parched."

Instinctively the servant moved to obey but Tuck laid a hand on her arm and shook his head.

"Oh, come now, friar. Are you going to make me die of thirst? Is that what the thick bailiff meant by his 'greenwood law'? You and I both know your case is built on quicksand. The sheriff will soon see me freed and I'll be back here as though nothing ever happened. You two men have made a very powerful enemy here today though, and I'll see you pay for this wrongful imprisonment."

"I still don't understand why he did it," Isabella said in a voice that sounded like it wouldn't hold out much longer without rest. "With no motive, Brother Tuck, your case is, as he says, going to crash about your ears."

"There *is* no motive," de Courcy crowed. "Unless you think I simply enjoy harming my wife, and I'm sure even the servants will agree that is untrue. I have never been anything but cordial to her. Eh, Anne? Isn't that right? Reynardine? Speak up you bastard, you were quick enough to answer the friar's questions!"

The servants' faces were pale as the understanding of their situation hit them but then Tuck spoke again.

"I have seen the will Lady Isabella's father left."

Now de Courcy's features turned ashen and he gaped in disbelief at Tuck. "You're lying. You can't just wander in off the street and demand to see a legal document that has nothing to do with you. You're not even a representative of the Crown!"

"What will?" Isabella appeared completely baffled by this latest twist in the tale, as did Little John.

"Remember I travelled to York?"

The bailiff nodded. "Aye. To see one of the bishops about exorcising a demon or something."

"No, I never said that, John. You just assumed that's what I was doing. Actually, I obtained a letter of authorization from Sir Henry de Faucumberg, which granted me access to the probate records for this parish. Specifically, the will that Lady Isabella's father left when he died."

De Courcy was silent now, tight lipped and fidgeting as if he wanted to explode and murder everyone in the room.

"You may remember," the friar said, turning once again to Isabella, "telling me that your father disliked Sir Adam and did not want you wed to him?"

"Of course," she agreed. "Father made no secret of his feelings, but he loved me and wouldn't stand in my way when I told him of my wish to marry. What does that have to do with anything?"

"Nothing—" de Courcy growled but John slapped him in the ear again and the nobleman buckled in agony.

"If you don't keep your mouth shut, I'll keep hitting you in that same ear until you're deaf, you little toad. Now be silent – I want to hear this."

De Courcy's eyes were damp with tears of pain and fury but his head was spinning and it was obvious John was deadly serious. He clenched his fists behind his back but didn't make another sound, allowing the friar to go on.

"Well, Sir Adam told us that he, on the contrary, was good friends with your father, which I found odd for both you, and the priest in Wakefield, had told me otherwise. Reynardine!"

The cook jerked upright, surprised to be addressed.

"Aye?"

"How long have you lived here in Croftun, serving Lady Isabella and her father before her?"

Reynardine hesitated, counting the years in his head before he shrugged and smiled ruefully. "I'm not sure, Brother Tuck. Forty years, perhaps."

"So, you remember your mistress setting fires as a child?" Tuck grinned. "Like that time she burned down the barn? That must have caused some consternation, eh?"

The old cook stared back at him in confusion, then his eyes narrowed as if he suspected a trick was being played on him.

"No barns have ever burned down in Croftun, that I'm aware of," he said firmly. "And the lady never started any fires either. I don't know where you got that idea from, but it's bloody nonsense."

"You lying dog," John growled, grasping Sir Adam by the front of his cloak. "You've led us wrong this whole time, trying to make us think your wife is possessed by some devil with your stories."

"Thankfully, your father was a wise man," Tuck said, nodding as he turned once more to Isabella. "Like Reynardine, he must have foreseen the type of person Sir Adam would turn out to be, and so he had written into his will certain stipulations."

"Like what?" the lady demanded.

"His estate was passed down to you," the friar replied. "But it was written into the will that Sir Adam, even as your husband, would not inherit anything if you, Lady Isabella, were to die within ten years of your betrothal. In such a case, your children, if you had any, would be the benefactors. The only way he," at this Tuck turned in disgust to their captive, "could inherit the entire estate was if you were declared unfit to manage it."

"You mean if I was mad."

"Exactly," Tuck confirmed. "If he could have you imprisoned for some heinous crime, or see you declared insane, or even if you were to take your own life as a result of some madness – everything would then pass to him. Look for yourself." He fished inside his robe and drew out the copy he'd made of the will in York, passing it to the lady, who unrolled the parchment and began to read.

Little John whistled and shook his head at the audacity of de Courcy's scheme. His appreciation didn't extend to compliments though. "You really are a bastard," he growled, and made as if to strike the nobleman on the head again, although this time he didn't land the blow. Seeing de Courcy squirm was satisfaction enough.

"How could this be legal?" Lady Isabella demanded. "I mean, yes, it all seems very clever on my father's behalf but...The law is not usually weighted in favour of a woman."

Tuck nodded. "You're right, of course. But your father was a very well-connected man. I don't know his history, but it seems he was friends with the previous king. Edward, second of the name, was a witness to the will and, as such, it is as legally binding as any document can be. And you knew all about it, didn't you, Sir Adam?"

Everyone turned to stare at the disgraced nobleman and even Anne had an angry expression on her face now. Any trace of respect or subservience had gone from both servants' eyes, but de Courcy glared back at them all with the arrogant defiance of a high-born man who believes the world was placed there for his sole benefit.

"This is nonsense," he spat. "Why would I go to all this trouble, when I have access to my wife's fortune already?"

"Simple greed," Tuck retorted. "You do not have full access to Lady Isabella's fortune, and neither does she as a result of the aforementioned clause. For now, she receives a monthly stipend until that tenth year of marriage has passed, and you must ask her approval to spend any of it. On that wine you enjoy so much, for example."

"That bloody wine," Isabella muttered, as if the expensive beverage had been a bone of contention in their marriage for a long time.

"Your words are empty and carry no weight, friar," de Courcy said, and a sneer tugged at the corner of his mouth. "This is all lies."

"Lies?" John laughed without humour. "Even if everything Tuck was saying about the will, and you carrying out the previous attacks, was untrue – you seem to forget I saw you with my own eyes, trussing up your wife like a prize chicken after choking her half to death. You then resisted my attempt to arrest you, coming at me with your sword!"

"We're going over old ground here," de Courcy muttered. "Let's just get this over with."

"What will happen now?" Lady Isabella asked, and exhaustion filled every word as she placed the copy of her father's will next to her on the couch.

"You don't have to worry anymore," John said, smiling reassuringly. "Your ordeal is over."

"Over?" She screwed up her face and looked like a frightened child, making Tuck's heart ache with sympathy. "Over, bailiff? It's just beginning! I will have to testify against my own husband, won't I? And like he says, he will get away with his crimes. The law will allow him to return here and live within my father's house as if it was his own, while I will live in fear, wondering what new crimes he'll perpetrate against me."

John opened his mouth to offer some encouraging platitude, but Isabella angrily raised a hand and broke in before he could utter a single word.

"Don't patronise me bailiff. Don't tell me you'll watch over me to make sure Adam doesn't harm me again. We know that is an impossible task."

The giant bailiff blinked and looked away, abashed, knowing she was correct. For all his size and skill at fighting, no-one would be able to protect Lady Isabella from her husband when he returned from trial.

"We will take him to Nottingham," Tuck said. "He'll spend some time in the castle cells, until the magistrates come, and he can be tried. Hopefully that will take a while."

"Could be months," John said, smiling nastily at de Courcy who sighed as if dealing with an unruly child.

"More likely the sheriff will see through this ludicrous story and set me free straight away," the nobleman retorted.

Tuck nodded. "It could be months, or it could be days before this is dealt with," he admitted to Isabella. "You might want to put measures in place to prepare for his return."

"Measures?" she demanded, and tears were in her eyes again as she glared at the friar fearfully.

"Hire a bodyguard," John suggested.

"And offer prayers to St Uncumber," Tuck said seriously. "Patron saint of women plagued by bad husbands. Perhaps she will help you, my lady."

De Courcy snorted in amusement, earning another smack about the ear from John, but Isabella covered her face in her hands and Tuck decided enough was enough for one day.

"Come on," he said to the bailiff. "We might as well start our journey to the city while it's still light. The sooner that piece of filth is away from Lady Isabella the better. Anne," he smiled at the serving girl who bowed her head in response. "Take good care of your mistress. A little warmed wine at regular intervals will do her good, and perhaps some chicken broth if Reynardine can manage it?"

"Of course," the old cook agreed enthusiastically, happy to have something to do that might ease the lady's discomfort. "I'll get some on the boil as soon as you're on your way to Nottingham, Brother Tuck."

"Good, thank you Reynardine. We'll be on our way then." The friar stood up and John opened the door, ushering his sour-faced captive out, into the hall. "Please try not to worry too much," Tuck said to Isabella as everyone exited the room. "God has a way of sorting these things out." Of course, he was a worldly man and knew God did no such thing at times, often allowing the wickedest of men to get away with their crimes unpunished, but the lady needed encouragement then, not cold, hard truths.

Her weak nod of farewell suggested she knew fine well that he was merely trying to give her the strength required to see out the coming days, but she appreciated his efforts, nonetheless.

"You'll need supplies, won't you?" Reynardine asked as John and Tuck walked towards the front door with his disgraced master. "If you're heading directly to Nottingham I mean. That's a fair distance, even on horseback."

"Aye, he's right," the bailiff said, hauling backwards on de Courcy's collar. "Unless we make a stop somewhere to buy food, and that'd just be an unnecessary delay."

"I can make you a couple of packs up in no time," the cook offered, drawing yet another sneer from de Courcy.

"All right," Tuck said. "The sooner we can reach Nottingham the better. I'd rather not have to look at that Godless devil any longer than necessary."

De Courcy opened his mouth to reply but John shoved him towards the door as Reynardine led the friar off to the kitchen.

"I'll meet you at the stables," Tuck called, but John was already outside and gone.

Reynardine proved true to his word and quickly threw some bread, cheese and salted meat into two rough sacks. These he handed to the friar before filling three ale skins and placing them in the largest of the sacks.

"That'll be enough to keep you going," the cook said, smiling in satisfaction. They clasped arms and then Reynardine turned away to bring down a battered old pot from a hook on the wall. "Godspeed, friend, and keep an eye on the master. He's a sly fox, as you well know. Lady Isabella should never have married him. Don't you worry about her now though, I'll take care of her – my broth is legendary."

Tuck grinned, for he could quite believe the cook's boast and then he made his way out into the cold afternoon air, drawing his cloak up around his neck as far as he could to keep out the draught.

"One last thing," Reynardine called after him. "What was the name of that saint you mentioned?"

"Uncumber," the friar shouted back, shivering and rubbing his hands together for warmth as the cold hit him. "Why?"

"I'll pray to her," the cook replied. "Once my broth starts to simmer. Lady Isabella will need all the help she can get to keep that bastard of a husband away from Croftun."

With a final wave, Tuck walked towards the stables, imagining how their trip would go. It was mid-afternoon now, so they'd be forced to camp out somewhere when it grew dark, which would mean taking turns to watch their prisoner. Tuck wasn't looking forward to that but there was no alternative – de Courcy would not hesitate to slit their throats if they relaxed their guard, and then somehow claim he'd done it in self-defence.

The nobleman really was a nasty piece of work, Tuck thought, feet crunching on the frost-encrusted grass as he neared his destination. To plan all this, and carry it out mercilessly over months, showed a calculating and cold mind, especially given how congenial Lady Isabella was.

He sighed heavily at the thought of the ruthless devil walking free and returning here to further terrorize his wife, but his silent exhalation quickly turned to a blasphemous oath more suited to a brigand than a man of God.

Galloping hard across the field ahead was Little John, bellowing threats as he chased another rider who could barely be made out in the distance.

The friar dropped his packs of supplies and ran for the stables, shouting for the young lad to make his mount ready, and fast.

It seemed Sir Adam de Courcy had somehow slipped free of his bonds and escaped.

CHAPTER FOURTEEN

Little John was furious – at himself as much as his escaped captive. When he'd tied up de Courcy by the riverside his fingers were numb from the cold and, clearly, he hadn't made a very good job of it. He was an experienced bailiff, never mind woodsman, and really should have redone the prisoner's bonds when they were inside and warmed up.

He kicked his heels into his mount again, urging it to run faster despite its heavy burden. His quarry seemed to be pulling away from him, no doubt due to the fact de Courcy was not only lighter, but a better rider. John couldn't let the bastard escape though – he would never live it down. And on top of that, of course, he wanted to make sure Lady Isabella had at least a few days' respite from her husband's brooding presence. John groaned as he imagined the frightened woman's reaction when she found out that the bailiff, despite his promises, had let Sir Adam get away.

"You'd be better letting me catch you now," he roared, voice carrying far across the silent, frozen land, but it was pointless. When did a fleeing criminal ever stop when a lawman ordered them to? "I'm going to beat the shit out of you properly this time, de Courcy, unless you give up!"

The nobleman was a fair distance ahead of him yet, even so, the gesture he made over his shoulder was clear enough and made the bailiff even angrier, if that was possible.

Cursing, John glanced back himself and saw Tuck coming after them. The friar was a surprisingly good horseman and, had their roles been reversed, perhaps Tuck might have stood a chance of catching up with de Courcy, but, as it was, he was too far off. There was no way he would overhaul their disappearing prisoner. The bailiff could hear the irate clergyman's shouts of recrimination however and, again, he mentally berated himself. Tuck had put so much effort into solving this mystery, and John had ruined everything.

When he'd shoved de Courcy through the front doors the nobleman had cursed him and promised vengeance. Little did John know, the diminutive nobleman had somehow loosened his bonds and, when the stables came close, de Courcy suddenly turned and punched the bailiff right between the legs.

Such an attack was, of course, a classic way to incapacitate a man and it had certainly slowed John, who bent over double as his captive sprinted off. The stable boy must have been expecting the visitors to leave at any moment for he'd already saddled the horses belonging to Tuck and John, meaning de Courcy was able to simply vault up onto one of them – the friar's as it turned out – and gallop to freedom.

The pain had faded a little as John ran after his charge but the motion of the horse was doing little to help and his rage was growing with every passing moment as they covered the hard ground – de Courcy had better pray he escaped, because John was in no mood to be lenient if he caught up with the duplicitous little shit.

Such an outcome was highly unlikely though. De Courcy was further away than ever and John's mount seemed incapable of going any faster. The nobleman had the advantage of knowing the terrain as well – this was his manor after all, or his wife's at least, and he knew every inch of it intimately, for he spent much of his time riding.

"Holy Mary, mother of God, please let me catch that bastard," John whispered, fingering the hilt of his sword as the ground ahead changed. Where it had been wide and open, it now grew rocky, with hidden dips and patches of dead foliage which would make it harder for the horses to traverse at speed. Especially given how frosty the grass was.

John's mount was a large palfrey, unused to a race such as this, and it really began to flag now. The bailiff couldn't blame it and, despite his frustration, refrained from kicking his heels in harder in a futile attempt to drag another drop of energy from the animal.

All he could do was watch as de Courcy widened the gap between them even further, and wait for Friar Tuck to come alongside him.

But Mother Mary must have been listening to John's prayer, for just then the nobleman's horse seemed to slip and stumble. Braying in fear, the animal went head over heels, sending de Courcy flying with a cry of terror.

"*Now!*" the bailiff roared in triumph, charging past boulders and leafless bushes with a renewed sense of purpose. "I have you, de Courcy!"

In truth, he half-expected the fugitive wouldn't get up quickly from such a high-velocity spill but, first the fallen horse rose on shaky legs, and then so did its rider. Both were dazed and looked around in shock, trying to get their bearings as John rode ever closer.

He didn't even draw his sword for de Courcy was still unarmed and little threat in a fight.

John's triumph quickly faded though, as he realised nothing had been gained. Aye, he would recapture his prisoner, and his reputation would remain intact – but, ultimately, Sir Adam de Courcy would face no real punishment for his crimes.

It would be better if the whoreson would fight back and I could end him for good, he thought, but Little John was no murderer. Although it might be truer justice than the law of the land would mete out, he would not kill an unarmed escapee. Even when he was an outlaw, John had been an honourable man who made sure other members of their gang never behaved too viciously.

Perhaps de Courcy didn't know all that. Perhaps the nobleman expected the enraged bailiff to beat him to death. Whatever his reasons, de Courcy had no intention of giving up just yet and he ran unsteadily towards his horse.

John had slowed his own mount by now, wary of falling down a hidden pothole himself, but Tuck, more confident despite riding a borrowed horse from the stables, galloped up beside him. They watched as the desperate nobleman stumbled towards his stolen animal which was still shaken from its tumble.

And they watched as the horse, startled once again by the staggering man approaching it, suddenly kicked out, catching Sir Adam de Courcy directly in the face with its iron-shod hooves.

CHAPTER FIFTEEN

Both Little John and Friar Tuck had seen men die horribly over the years. Indeed, they had been the ones to send many of them to their doom – killing and dying on the end of a sword was an occupational hazard when one was an outlaw after all.

Even so, both drew back in horror, aghast, as de Courcy was sent flying by the horse's kick, skull cracked like an eggshell on the side of one of Reynardine's kitchen pots.

For a long moment neither man moved, they simply stared at the limp body of the nobleman, half expecting him to get up and try to escape again. Of course, he didn't and, eventually, Tuck led the way to the downed fugitive, where he knelt and muttered a soft prayer, breath clouding in the freezing air.

God would be the judge of Sir Adam de Courcy now.

"At least Lady Isabella doesn't have to worry about his shit any more," John said grimly as he came up behind the friar. "I'd say everything's turned out for the best. St Uncumber must have been watching after all."

Tuck slowly got to his feet, wincing as his knee protested painfully, but he didn't reply to the bailiff's comment. He agreed with John's observation, but it seemed wrong to celebrate a man's death just moments after it had happened. Even someone as unsavoury as Sir Adam de Courcy.

Slowly, cautiously, the clergyman walked towards his horse – the one stolen by the nobleman.

The one that had just killed the nobleman.

Tuck spoke to it in a calm voice and its eyes bulged, nostrils flaring as he approached, almost as if the beast understood the magnitude of its actions. It knew its master though, for Tuck had been kind to it over the years, and it allowed him to come close enough to grasp the reins and stroke its smooth neck reassuringly.

"It's probably best if we let this fine fellow walk back to the house unburdened," the friar decided, nodding towards the spare horse he'd ridden there himself on. "Toss de Courcy's body over that one, John. We'll take him home for burial."

"That's very noble of you," the giant bailiff said, quickly moving to carry out his friend's command. "To walk all the way back to the house, I mean, just so your horse doesn't have to carry you."

Tuck snorted with sardonic laughter, eyes twinkling as he sauntered past John. "Me? Walk? I'm taking *your* horse, you daft bastard. My knee is playing up again!"

* * *

Four days later, Tuck and John met once more in the alehouse in Wakefield. It had taken that long to get everything tidied up following the arrest, and subsequent death, of Sir Adam de Courcy. First, of course, they had to break the 'sad' news to Lady

Isabella, and then decide what was to be done with the body.

Isabella did not want her husband's shade haunting her in death as he had done in life, so begged them to place the corpse in one of the storehouses on the estate, until the coroner could come and examine it. The formalities of law had to be followed, of course, so, unfortunately, they couldn't just bury the dead man and be done with it. Not yet, at least.

So they had, as respectfully as possible, deposited Sir Adam's body in a tool-shed within the estate but out of sight of the manor house itself, and then they said their goodbyes, wished the lady good fortune, and rode to Nottingham to make their report to the sheriff.

Sir Henry de Faucumberg knew Little John very well, and he had listened intently as the whole story was recounted. Then he thanked the bailiff and friar for their service to the crown, rewarded them with a bag of coins, and let them return to their homes.

"What do you think the lady will do now?" John asked, wiping ale from his beard. "Once de Courcy's funeral is over I mean."

"Remarry?" Tuck mused. "She's still quite young, very pretty, and childless. Rich too. I expect there will be no shortage of suitors."

John shook his head sadly. "I hope she finds someone better than the last one. I still can't believe he was so devious. Why not just be content with what he had?"

Tuck shrugged and lifted another piece of cheese from the trencher the landlord had placed before them when they came in. "Some people are never happy."

"He had everything a man could wish for though," the bailiff persisted. "Money, a beautiful wife who was years younger than himself, land, servants…"

The pair sat in thoughtful silence, contemplating the collective madness of humanity, and then John grinned.

"The sheriff was impressed with how you solved the mystery, my friend," he said. "So was I, truth be told. We make a good team."

Tuck nodded, smiling beatifically. "True. I have the brains, and the brawn, and the looks, and you…" He frowned, as if unable to think of a single quality of John's. "Actually, I'm not sure what you're good for. You're certainly no use at tying up prisoners." He laughed at his companion's hurt expression, then yelped and dodged backwards, away from the bailiff's blow.

"Seriously, though," John said once Tuck had stopped sniggering. "If you hadn't been with me that first time we visited Croftun, Lady Isabella would likely be dead by now, while her husband inherited her estate. You do have a knack of seeing things others would miss."

Tuck beamed, genuinely pleased by the compliment, and they ate and drank in silence, enjoying the cooking smells, the warmth from the fire, and the friendly, familiar atmosphere within the room.

"If we get a chance, we should do it again."

Tuck looked up, eyebrows drawn together in a frown. "Do what again?"

"Solve a mystery!" John said. "It's certainly more interesting than the usual work I do as a bailiff."

Tuck lifted his ale mug and sipped happily. Thoughtfully.

"Aye," he muttered, more to himself than John. "Maybe we should."

Just then the front door swung open, and a freezing draught blew through the place, turning every head towards the newcomer.

"Hurry up and shut the door, you fool," someone called from a shadowy corner. "It's bloody freezing in here."

"Shut the door?" the newcomer retorted, pointing threateningly into the corner that the voice had come from. "You better shut your *mouth*, Alfred, you old prick, or I'll knock that last remaining tooth of yours right down your scrawny throat."

The patrons of the alehouse exploded in hoots of laughter at the exchange and Tuck shook his head ruefully. Time had not softened Will Scaflock's temper much.

Their old friend spotted them near the hearth and, grinning, came over to join them.

"Hello, ladies," he said, sitting down and waving to the landlord for three more drinks. "You look serious. Anything I can help you with?"

"Aye," Tuck replied, jerking his head in John's direction. "You can teach him how to tie a knot."

THE END

If you enjoyed *Faces of Darkness* **please** leave a review on Amazon and/or Goodreads.
Every single one really helps me out, and they are all HUGELY appreciated.

Also, if you'd like a **FREE** Forest Lord short story, sign up for my [EMAIL LIST](www.stevenamckay.com) at www.stevenamckay.com and get "The Rescue" delivered straight to your inbox. I regularly run competitions to win signed books and Audible downloads and I promise not to spam you constantly.

Thank you so much for reading!
Steven

Author's Note

If you follow me, you'll probably know that I had no plans to ever write another Forest Lord book. As much as I loved the characters, I simply wanted to move on with my new **Warrior Druid of Britain** series and explore other things like my standalone novel *Lucia*.

But then I listened to a podcast (Strange Matters) about a very weird unsolved mystery from the 1980s which really grabbed my attention, and I started to think it might make a good base for a historical fiction tale. In real life, Canadian nurse Cindy James was apparently stalked for years, suffering horrific mental and physical abuse until, ultimately, she was found dead with her hands and feet tied together behind her back. The authorities ruled it a *suicide*, concluding that she had been torturing herself all along.

To be fair, the police had tried hard to find her tormentor, and Cindy even hired a private investigator to help. But no one ever saw the stalker, all leads fizzled out, and any time the police watched her house the attacks stopped until they'd left.

Did she kill herself? There's an audio recording of an answerphone message her ex-husband received from the apparent stalker which you can find online – it simply says, "Cindy. Dead meat. Soon." It's even creepier than it reads, as the caller spoke in a guttural voice that really makes the hairs on the listener's neck rise. And yet, to me, it's a woman's voice on the recording, not a man, so maybe she *was* behind it all.

There have, of course, been some famous cases of "multiple personality disorder" as it was known back then. The book and movie *Sybil* was based on the apparent experiences of a woman who had a multitude of different people inside her, although it was later claimed to be total fiction. Then there was Ruth Finley, who suffered in a similar way to Cindy James. Finley received death threats written in the form of poetry, eggs and faeces were thrown at her house, her phone lines were cut, and she was even stabbed three times. Yet it turned out she was doing it all to herself, as she eventually admitted.

In contrast, to me the most haunting aspect of Cindy James's case is the fact that it remains unsolved. I knew if I was to base a novella on her ordeal it *had* to have a resolution, and it had to have a 'happy' ending, with some form of justice for the victim.

Researching all of this creeped me out so much that I had to move from my usual writing spot in my study, with an open door at my back, to a seat where I could see all around so no-one could sneak up on me! But our heroes in *Faces of Darkness* aren't frightened of shadows the way I am. I thought this mystery was ideal for Friar Tuck to investigate, and who better as a sidekick than Little John, who'd been a bailiff beside Robin Hood in *Blood of the Wolf*?

With any luck, Lady Isabella de Courcy, unlike Cindy James, was left to enjoy her life in peace once her tormentor was out of the picture…

I really enjoyed writing *Faces of Darkness* and I hope you had fun reading it. If you did, **please leave a review on Amazon** – if people like this novella I *might* just write some more with Tuck and John investigating other, similar cases drawn from the weird podcasts I listen to while out at my day job…

Steven A. McKay
Old Kilpatrick
October 20th, 2019

ALSO BY STEVEN A. MCKAY & ACKNOWLEDGEMENTS

The Forest Lord Series:

Wolf's Head
The Wolf and the Raven
Rise of the Wolf
Blood of the Wolf

Knight of the Cross
Friar Tuck and the Christmas Devil
The Rescue and Other Tales
The Abbey of Death

Warrior Druid of Britain Chronicles:

The Druid
Song of the Centurion

Lucia (an AUDIBLE exclusive!)

Acknowledgements

Thanks to my mum for beta reading and pointing out any glaring errors and my wife Yvonne for a few great suggestions on how to make the book better.

LUCIA

What makes life worth living for a slave of Rome? The promise of vengeance, no matter how long it takes.

For Lucia, who was taken from her home in Germania as a child, most days are, at best, drudgery, at worst, a waking nightmare. As she and her friends are used and abused, bought and sold, day after day from cradle to grave, the slave-girl wonders how they all survive without going mad, or murdering their owner, Tribune Publius Licinius Castus. For him the women are mere playthings and both sexes nothing more than tools to work his sprawling estate.

Yet Villa Tempestatis, with its picturesque surroundings in Britannia's green countryside, offers a life that's a little easier than elsewhere in the Roman empire. The slaves form strong bonds of love and friendship, enjoy feasts and holiday celebrations together, and are even allowed, sometimes, to start a family. Many of them are happy enough with their lot.

Despite that, every moment of Lucia's life is blighted by her hate for the master and his cruel manageress Paltucca, and only seeing them both destroyed will bring her a measure of peace, even if it takes decades of work and planning…

This standalone novel from the bestselling author of *The Druid* tells a tale of love and hate, revenge and redemption, that's quite different to anything you've ever read before.

OUT NOW – ONLY FROM AUDIBLE

Printed in Great Britain
by Amazon